"I know this mountain chalet,"

Dimitri said. "We can sneak up there and spend the night. The whole night, till dawn."

Winnie got goosebumps. It wasn't like Dimitri would show her to the guest room and give her a good night kiss on the cheek. "You mean you have a friend who'll lend you the key?" she asked.

Dimitri gave her one of his lopsided, sexy smiles. "I can 'borrow' the key. No problem. How does nine o'clock sound? I'll tell you where to meet me."

Before she could even think what she was going to answer, he was kissing her again—long, slow kisses that made her feel all bubbly.

Tomorrow night, she'd really wanted to go to Spring Formal with Josh. But she had to face it—Josh just was not there for her anymore. She couldn't count on him.

"Sure, that sounds fabulous. I'd love to," Winnie said.

Don't miss these books
in the exciting FRESHMAN DORM
series

FRESHMAN HEARTBREAK

LINDA A. COONEY

HarperPaperbacks
A Division of HarperCollinsPublishers

HarperPaperbacks *A Division of* HarperCollins*Publishers*
10 East 53rd Street, New York, N.Y. 10022

Copyright © 1992 by Linda Alper and Kevin Cooney
All rights reserved. No part of this book may be used or reproduced in any manner whatsoever without written permission of the publisher, except in the case of brief quotations embodied in critical articles and reviews. For information address HarperCollins*Publishers,*
10 East 53rd Street, New York, N.Y. 10022.

Cover art by Tony Greco

First printing: February 1992

Printed in the United States of America

HarperPaperbacks and colophon are trademarks of HarperCollins*Publishers*

10 9 8 7 6 5 4 3 2 1

One

"The three of us used to take hours deciding what to wear back in high school," Winnie Gottlieb said as she paced nervously alongside the window in Faith Crowley's dorm room.

There was a half frown on Winnie's face as she watched Faith try on and discard one piece of clothing after another. Meanwhile, Winnie's other high-school best friend, KC Angeletti, sat on Faith's bed fastening a little dress-for-success tie around the collar of her starched blouse. All three of them were now freshman at the University of Springfield and were getting ready for a Sunday dorm picnic.

"I guess some things don't change," Winnie went on.

Faith smiled and finished weaving her blond hair into a French braid. Then she reached in her dresser drawer and pulled out a pair of worn, pink Osh-Kosh's. But instead of pulling the overalls on, she tossed them to Winnie. "Here, Win," she said. "Since you're reminiscing about high school, you can wear these. They're the ones I wore when I worked backstage for the senior musical."

"That's okay." Winnie flipped them to KC instead. "They aren't exactly my style." She tugged on her earring, which was shaped like a refrigerator, then respiked her short, dark hair.

"These aren't exactly my style either," KC commented as she pretended to take off her Tri Beta sorority pin and attach it to the overall pocket. "I can't believe you still wear your old high-school clothes," she teased Faith. "Some things may be the same, but I feel like I've changed so much since high school that I can barely remember who the old KC Angeletti was."

"The old KC was gorgeous and ambitious. She wanted to get her MBA, make tons of money, and travel the world. Kind of exactly the way you are now," Winnie joked.

KC laughed. "Except that now I'm in love, too.

I'm actually going to leave U of S to go study in Europe—just so I can be with Peter."

"Poor KC," Faith sang.

"Yeah, really," Winnie agreed. "I'll miss you, KC, but I don't exactly feel sorry for you."

KC sat up on the bed, her posture as perfect as ever. "I'm not sure that this move is going to help my future career, though," she said. "I mean, it won't hurt my career—but I'm leaving midsemester, right after Spring Formal. I'm leaving the both of you and my sorority. I never thought I'd be so in love that my priorities would change. But Peter comes first."

"I suppose we've all changed," Winnie said. She was certainly different from the small-town Winnie who'd flitted from one guy to another with no promises, no commitments. Back then everything had been easy. Of course, she hadn't known Josh Gaffey in high school. She hadn't been in love. Now she was a college freshman and involved in a wonderful, mature relationship. But if it was all so wonderful and mature, why did it also suddenly feel so stifling, so predictable, so, so, B.O.R.I.N.G?

Winnie wished she knew. She began to pace again. "Isn't it amazing. *I* used to be the one to do exciting things like going to Europe," she chattered. "Now I just cram for tests, study little white mice in the psych lab, and watch Josh play Crystal

Quest on his computer." She bit her fingernail. "My big thrill these days is watching old *Star Trek* reruns with Josh in the lobby of my dorm."

"Sounds exciting," said KC.

"Hey, I always liked those Klingons," added Faith.

"At least we have this picnic and hayride today," Winnie reminded herself. "And Spring Formal is coming up. Even Josh can't take a computer to Spring Formal."

"I wouldn't put it past him," Faith teased.

"That's right, Win," KC joined in. "You never know."

Did anyone ever really know anything? Winnie wondered. In the past she'd gone way overboard just to figure things out. Going over the edge had made her feel that she was alive. She was starting to crave that vital feeling now. But why? Just when she and Josh had reached an incredibly stable, safe place in their relationship, why was she starting to fantasize about dying her hair orange and piercing a ring through her nose? She leaned toward Faith's window and yelled out to the dorm green. "DOES ANYBODY REALLY KNOW ANYTHING?"

"I know you, Win," Faith reassured her. She came over and slipped her arm around Winnie's shoulders. "You're wild and loony. And you're known for wearing your underwear on the outside of your clothes."

"At least I'm known for something other than being attached to Josh," Winnie grumbled. "Winnie and Josh. U of S freshman couple of the year. Not only do they live in the same dorm—on the same floor—they eat the same junk food and finish one another's sentences." She forced herself to stop talking and looked out the window again. "We're probably starting to look alike, too. All we need now is a shaggy dog and we'll be completely indistinguishable."

Faith clipped her overalls over a lacy white T-shirt. "Hey! Speaking of dogs, I have to tell you the latest horror story with my *dear* roommate, Liza Ruff."

KC looked around the room. "Where is Liza, Roommate from Elm Street?"

Faith giggled. "I think her middle name *is* Freddy. She's probably at the theater, doing extra rehearsals for *Macbeth*. She's playing a witch. Surprise, surprise."

"Typecasting," said KC, pointing to Liza's half of the room.

Winnie surveyed the room, too. Half of it was amazingly organized—Faith's half—while Liza's half was strewn with sparkly tights, leopard-print stretch pants, theatrical photos, records, candles, and a giant bag of dog kibble. Coleridge Hall was the creative-arts dorm and Faith and Liza were both drama majors, but the similarity ended there. Faith was the backstage, no-job-is-too-small type, while showy Liza wanted to be a star.

"Actually, I'm trying not to let Liza bug me," Faith said. She faced Liza's half of the room and covered her eyes. "I have to keep reminding myself of my new approach. I'm going to keep cool, not get uptight, stay in the moment, and just deal with things as they come up."

"Hmm," KC said with mock seriousness. "Could this new attitude possibly be inspired by Scott Sills?"

Faith blushed. Scott was a jock on the U of S volleyball team. He was about as carefree and in the moment as it was possible to be. Since meeting Scott, Faith had learned to loosen up and not take things so seriously. "Could be," Faith replied, gloating.

KC tossed a pillow at her.

Winnie didn't want to think about dependable, straight Faith letting loose with Scott. Neither did she want to think about KC going to Europe just because Peter had won a photography scholarship. "Why did you say 'speaking of dogs'?" she reminded Faith, hoping to change the subject. "What does Liza have to do with dogs?"

"Yeah," KC said. She stood up and pointed to the bag of dog food that sat between Liza's make-up box and her tape player. "What's with the puppy chow?"

"Liza has adopted a canine friend—against dorm rules," Faith complained. "And let's just say I like living with barking Max about as much as I like living with Liza."

"But you used to love dogs," Winnie said.

"Well. I guess I've changed since high school, too, because I am beginning to hate Max. He chewed up that book bag my parents gave me as a starting college present."

"Oh, no!" KC sympathized.

"Oh, yes. He completely destroyed it. I'm trying not to get freaked out about it." Faith suddenly froze. Her eyes darted to the door. "Don't look now. But I think you're about to meet the beast in person."

"In person? You mean in beastdom," Winnie corrected. She stared as Faith walked to the door and stood against it. Whining and the clip, clip of dog nails could be heard from the other side.

"Max, I know you're out there," Faith called. "Are you armed and dangerous? I'm only going to let you in for a second. We have a picnic to go to. Okay, I'm opening up," she warned. Then she turned the knob and the door flew back against the wall.

Even Winnie stepped back as a big, tan Labrador barged through the doorway, jumping into the room as if it were in the midst of a steeple chase. He bounded, barked, and drooled.

"Max!" Faith objected when Max jumped on her.

Max lunged at Winnie next, then leaped onto KC, leaving paw marks on her pleated skirt.

"MAX!" Faith hollered. She lunged for Max, but he scurried under Liza's bed, then lay there panting at her. "Thank you so much, Liza. And Lauren Turnbull-Smythe, where are you when I need you?" she pleaded to her invisible, first roommate, who had had to move off campus when she'd run out of money.

Winnie got down on her hands and knees and tried to coax Max out from under the bed. In a moment Faith was on the floor, helping her.

"Come on, Max," Faith cooed with forced sweetness. She looked at Winnie, then tried to calm herself down. "Like Scott says, just stay in the moment, keep cool, and everything will work out."

When Max was finally out from under the bed,

Winnie held him while Faith pulled on her old cowboy boots and the fringed Daniel Boone jacket Winnie and KC had given her for a sweet-sixteen present.

Max jumped up, nipping at the fringe on Faith's jacket. Faith lost her cool again. "Don't even think about it, Max. My book bag was bad enough. You destroy this jacket and you're . . . dog meat."

"Faith!" KC said laughing. "Now that really is a new you."

Faith began to laugh, too, an out-of-control, old high-school giggle. "I know. I'm a new, *mean* Faith."

"Not to Scott, I hope," KC said.

Faith gave out a silly shriek. "Never to Scott!"

The two of them burst out laughing again. Meanwhile, Winnie held Max and frowned. Maybe the new Faith could afford not to take things seriously. And maybe the new KC was so in love and hopeful that she didn't even mind Max jumping on her skirt. But Winnie wasn't finding anything very funny. She could only think about Max devouring everything in *her* room. Maybe then Josh would tear himself away from his computer long enough to help rescue her things. It was a pathetic fantasy, Winnie realized. Pretty soon she'd be daydreaming about knights and white horses.

Faith finally took Max and started tugging him

toward the door. "Let's go to the picnic. Maybe I can lose this four-footed stray along the way. At least I can get him out of here before I get caught for breaking another dorm rule. Come on, you two, let's find Scott, Peter, and Josh and go to the picnic."

KC dodged Max and went into the hall. "I'll go get Peter downstairs. He's probably developing some pictures in the darkroom. He has to finish two big assignments in order to transfer any credits from this semester. See you on the hayride." She waved briefly and raced to the stairwell, nearly colliding with two dance majors who were doing stretching exercises in the corridor.

"C'mon, Winnie," Faith said as Max pulled her down the hall. "You can pick up Josh and I'll find Scott before he uses up all the picnic plates as Frisbees."

Winnie hesitated for a minute. Then she took a breath and headed back over to Forest Hall.

"It's time to go, Josh."

Winnie stood in Josh's open doorway, waiting for him to turn around and rush over to hug her. But Josh didn't want to take his eyes off his computer screen.

"Yoohoooo," Winnie tried again. "Remember me?"

At last the hunched shoulders relaxed. "Huh?" Josh turned around to face her. "Do I know you?" he teased. "Have I ever seen you before?"

Winnie walked in. "Good question."

Josh fingered his single blue earring. As soon as Winnie was close enough, he pulled her onto his lap and she touched the woven twine bracelet he always wore on his right wrist. As he took her for a turn in his swivel chair she held on by gripping the cuffs of his gray sweatshirt.

"I've missed you," Josh said. Then he reached past her to type on his keyboard again. His chin dug into her shoulder.

"You have?" She looked back and tried to meet his green eyes, but he was focused on the screen.

"If you're gone an hour, I miss you," he said, without looking up.

Winnie stared at the numbers and letters as they raced across the screen. Then she leaned back against his chest, taking in the familiar smell and feel of him. "Almost done?" she asked.

"Not quite."

"Well, the picnic starts in about five minutes."

He typed faster. "It does?"

"It does," she repeated. "There are games and food and a hayride. We're going. Together. Remember?"

"Uh-hmm," he muttered in a way that let her know he didn't remember at all.

"Josh?"

"Hmm." He had that preoccupied air that told her that he wasn't even really listening. He was just tuned into those keys and the fascinating figures up on the screen.

"Josh!" Winnie said, grabbing his hands so that he couldn't type anymore. "Stop. It's time to leave. Exit. Erase. Do not pass Go. Detach, or whatever the computer calls it." She got up from his lap and spun his chair around so that he had to look at her.

"Right, right. But just one more second, Win." Josh swiveled back to face the screen and replaced the floppy in the drive for another. He punched in a series of mysterious codes and then the machine took over and started chugging off by itself. He looked at Winnie. "Sorry," he said. "This project is driving me nuts. I can't wait until it's done."

"Tell me about it!" Winnie exploded. She stood in front of his roommate Mikoto's bed and glared down at him. "Okay. Just give me a yes or no answer. Are you going to the picnic or not?"

Josh finally ran a hand through his hair and sighed. "If I don't fix this by tonight, I'll never get it done, Win. But look, after you come back from the picnic, stop by and I'll take a break. We can go sit in the dorm lounge and watch TV. How's that?"

"I take it that means no. What about Spring Formal," she reminded him. "Are you going to forget about that, too?"

Josh really looked at her. "Spring Formal?" Suddenly he was the old Josh, the Josh who left love notes on her door, who was always there when she needed him.

Winnie connected with his eyes and smiled. She knelt down and reached for him, but a jumble of buzzing and the flash of tiny lights stopped her.

Josh looked at his computer again. "I can't believe this!" he cried. "Thirty-five more clusters. I hope I saved those statistics on a floppy."

Something inside Winnie suddenly felt so completely smothered. She wasn't about to lie down and weep, though. She simply wanted to scream and throw things. But the only things to throw were Mikoto's premed books or Josh's computer. Without another word she stomped toward the door.

Josh didn't look up. As loudly as her brain was screaming, *Stop me. Talk to me. I'm going to do something crazy,* he didn't hear her.

"Be sure to let me know when your clusters reformat and your floppies stand up straight," she said when she reached the hall.

Josh just waved his hand, as if she'd told him to have a nice day.

Winnie thought about slamming his door shut. But she didn't. Instead she walked quietly back to her room. She didn't want to do anything that was even a tiny bit extreme. Because once she got started, it was hard for her to stop.

Two

*L*auren Turnbull-Smythe wasn't getting ready for the picnic. She was rubbing her hands on the apron that covered her poufy red skirt and slipping the embroidered suspenders a little higher on her shoulders. "It's so hard to clean in this uniform," she grumbled. "I waste so much time pushing up these dumb straps."

There seemed to be miles of ballroom floor still left to go over and her vision swam as she looked across the parquet and wondered how she would ever get to the other side. It was like the Sahara Desert—endless, and without an oasis in sight.

"I can't take this anymore," Lauren mumbled. "With what the Springfield Mountain Inn pays me, I might as well be a slave."

But she couldn't afford to quit. This was the only job Lauren had been qualified for after her mother, in a fit over the fact that Lauren refused to pledge Tri Beta, the top sorority on campus, would no longer pay to keep her in college. Mrs. Turnbull-Smythe had even gone ahead and frozen Lauren's trust fund. Nevertheless, Lauren was determined to stay at U of S, although it wasn't easy being down on her hands and knees in the Powder Ballroom, scrubbing away so that all the U of S students going to the Spring Formal next week could have a lovely time. She herself wasn't going to the dance, not since she'd broken up with her boyfriend, Dash Ramirez. Instead, she'd be putting in overtime. She'd be folding sheets and cleaning overflowing toilets while everyone else had a great time.

"Lauren! Hey!"

She looked up, squinting. Why couldn't she see straight? Hard work seemed to be taking its toll. Not only was her vision getting worse, but her delicate soft hands were now red and hardened. The only positive change was that her plump shape had been whittled away to a leaner, shaplier form. Her eyes finally focused and there was no doubt who was walking toward her. It was Dash.

"I thought I might find you here," Dash said, coming to a stop in front of her. "Looks like you're working hard." His long dark hair was uncombed, and he plucked at the red bandanna around his neck. He had on a clean T-shirt, but the ink on his fingers gave him away. As a reporter at the U of S *Weekly Journal,* he spent so much of his time in the newspaper office that he claimed to have *ink* in his *inkstream.* But even though the old Dash was familiar to Lauren, there was no way to feel comfortable about seeing him. After all, they hadn't spoken for days.

"Look," Dash said, "I don't want to bother you, but I brought you . . . um . . . Well, when you get a chance, here's my next article for the column." He pulled out a few sheets of paper from his pocket along with a battered Swiss army knife.

"Oh, you mean, for the next *His and Hers* piece?"

"Right." He rather self-consciously put back the knife. "Since we're cowriting this column for the paper, I wanted you to see my topic for the second installment ASAP. But if you're too busy—"

"I'll read it as soon as I get off duty," Lauren answered.

"Great," Dash said. "Next time you can choose the topic."

Lauren nodded and stuck the pages in the pocket of her apron.

"Hope you don't mind, but I showed it to Greg already," Dash went on. Greg Sukimaki was editor of the *Weekly Journal* and Dash valued his editorial judgment above anyone else's.

"Not at all. I expect you to show him anything before me. You did it the last time." Lauren's violet eyes flashed as she drove her point home.

"Now, just what do you mean by that?" Dash snapped. Lauren could see him clench his fists inside his pants pockets.

"All I meant was . . . well, you kind of went all over the place in our first column about male-and-female friendships," Lauren answered, trying to discuss only the facts since everything else seemed off limits.

"It worked, didn't it? I say things in print that I mean."

"Well, so do I!" Lauren blurted out.

"Hey, I know you do. You just didn't understand what I was getting at."

Dash looked upset. He was going to leave. Lauren was sure of it. And even though she was mad, she didn't want him to go. "So how is everything at the paper these days?" she asked, desperately trying to forget her anger and to think of something bright to say.

Dash shrugged. "Well, Greg's gone soft in the head. He wants to start a cooking column. He's trying to find somebody who has great recipes that require only a can opener and a hot plate. You know, 'How to Eat for a Year Without Going Near a Stove.' "

Lauren wondered how he could be funny when she felt so terrible. "I could manage that one, I guess. You should see some of the things I've dished up in my apartment lately."

Dash nodded. It was silent in the ballroom again.

"Well—" they both said at once.

Lauren felt her toes curl up inside her sneakers. She didn't understand how she could be at a loss for words with someone she had been so in love with until a few days ago. Dash looked around as if he were trying to find a new subject, too.

"You're sure cleaning this place up," he finally observed. "It's more than those of us going to Spring Formal deserve."

"Does that mean you're going to the dance?" she asked.

Dash looked at her as though she'd spoken in a foreign language, then he shrugged, shifted his weight, and cleared his throat. "Maybe, I don't know."

"I guess you've got too much work."

"Well, um, that's not it exactly," he faltered, "I mean if I finish my columns, and if there's nothing better to do, yes, I might like to go."

Lauren tried to read his expression. Did that mean he'd like to go with someone in particular? And if so, who? And did he take her question as an invitation—because naturally, she hadn't meant it to sound that way. But then just what *did* she mean?

Lauren suddenly got the feeling that neither one of them knew. Dash seemed to read her mind. "Well, I'm glad I found you. I'll see you around," he said, nervously adjusting his bandanna. "Let me know what you think of my article. I'll read your piece . . . whenever."

"Thanks."

Dash half smiled, then turned around. Lauren watched him walk across the floor, getting farther and farther away. Without thinking, she stood up and took a step toward him, accidentally kicking her bucket, so that dirty water sloshed in all directions.

"What's going on?" head maid Gladys Baker barked as she came rushing through a doorway. "Aren't you finished yet?"

"Well, I was just going over a few spots that—"

"These puddles are unacceptable. We can't leave any wet spots in here."

Lauren tuned Gladys out. She allowed her mind to float back to Winter Formal, back to that wonderful night when it hadn't mattered at all that she was a maid. It had been a perfect evening for her, even though it was perfectly rotten for everyone else she knew. Winnie and KC had been fighting like ocelots. In a fit of rage, Winnie had shoved KC in the Inn's swimming pool. It was incredible—neither one got to dance with the guy they had intended to be with. But for Lauren, everything had worked out. She'd seen Dash and exchanged a few casual words with him. He'd been lost in thought, and they'd been walking down the hall together, when suddenly he'd pulled her to him. He'd pressed her close in an embrace she'd dreamed of her entire life. The kiss had melted them together.

Gladys blew her nose angrily and the sound woke Lauren from her daydream. "So are you going to just stand there, or are you going to clean this mess up?" Gladys demanded.

Lauren was still kissing Dash in her mind when she answered. "I'll clean it up," she said automatically.

Angrily, she stuck her mop in the pail and then began sloshing the floor.

Three

T he dorm picnic was in full swing. There were dozens of students all over the green playing guitars, tossing Frisbees, doing daredevil tricks on skateboards, as well as preparing themselves for the FLYING BLACK SEED CONTEST, otherwise known as the Watermelon Wipeout.

"Ewwww! Gross-out. Watermelon seeds."

"Nature's flying black flatheads."

"The bigger the mouth, the better the blast."

"No, the poutier the lips, the more explosive the projection."

"Hey, have you ever seen Barney do this? He

can fire them off like a machine gun."

"Ewwww, gross-out."

"Sick."

"What is this? Like totally whacko or something?"

You bet it is! Faith felt like shouting. *And I'm loving every second of it.* She giggled and grabbed her own piece of watermelon. Every time she and Scott looked at each other with the big watermelon rinds posed before their mouths, they cracked each other up.

"On your mark, get set! Dig in!" yelled the contest organizer.

Scott chomped down on his huge piece of watermelon, and Faith, barely able to stop giggling, did the same. She spit her seeds out and took another huge mouthful.

"Let's go. You've gotta do better than that!" Scott said, wiping his mouth on the sleeve of his green-and-white-striped rugby shirt. He shook his shaggy, sun-bleached hair out of his eyes. "I won the potato-sack race and squeaked ahead of you in the egg-in-the-spoon contest, and I'm going to beat you again if you don't watch out."

"*You* watch out," Faith bantered back. "I'm ahead." Faith chewed fast and swallowed. A few students who'd been watching them started cheering her on.

"Hey," Scott grumbled good-naturedly. "I think she's winning."

"I am!" Faith nearly choked as she spoke, but she kept on eating and spitting out seeds. She could do it, she was sure of it. How weird to think that a watermelon-eating competition at the dorm picnic could be so much plain old fun. The old Faith, the steady girlfriend who used to go with Brooks Baldwin in high school, would have stood aside and commented, "No thanks, that's too silly." But Scott got her to do crazy things, and she loved it. Of course, sometimes things could go too far, like when he'd talked her into carrying a fake ID so she could order a beer at The Pub. Still, Faith felt like being around Scott was good for her.

She was down to the rind and stole a quick glance at Scott, who still had a lot of pink left on his piece. Taking the last bite, she held her hands up in a gesture of triumph.

"We have a winner!" declared the organizer. Everyone cheered.

Scott put down his piece and reached for a napkin. With a grin that put two stunning dimples in his cheeks, he tenderly wiped Faith's mouth and face. Then he scrubbed her nose for good luck and planted a kiss on it.

"You faker! You really are a party girl!" he said.

"You're right!" Faith glowed inside, wondering why it had taken her all this while to let loose and enjoy herself. She flopped down onto the grass, and Scott did the same.

"Listen," Faith said, "would you like to go to the spring formal with me?"

She had a momentary pang as soon as she said the words, because she had never been so carefree and brave before in her life. But when she saw the relaxed smile on Scott's face, she knew she hadn't flubbed it.

"Hey, I would love to go with you!" Scott said, rolling over and doing a back flip. "I mean, you probably think I'm an idiot for not asking you—"

"Oh, no!" Faith protested. She didn't want it to seem like she'd expected it.

"Faith, honest, I would have except I'm still not sure whether I'll be around. It's my volleyball team, you know—we're starting a series of out-of-town games, and next Saturday afternoon's a biggie."

"I see." Faith knew how much the games meant to him.

"So if we win it, we'll play another team in the division right near that town Saturday night."

There had been a time when Faith would have

been so disappointed, she would have curled into a shell for about a week. She'd actually stopped seeing Scott for a while because she felt their relationship wasn't planned and sensible enough. But over time she'd figured out that if she was having fun, what difference did it make why or how?

"Sure, that's okay with me," she said, hoping to sound totally devil-may-care about the whole thing.

Scott drew his powerful arm back, miming a volleyball serve. "Well, you never know. If we goof up, I'll be back here, and we'll take off for the formal and *par-r-ty*." He pulled on her braid, making it into a mustache under her nose. "You mind just keeping it up in the air?"

Faith shook her head, pushing the braid away so she could talk. "Actually, it's perfect. I'm going to have a killer week, and if I don't have to make fancy plans for the formal, it's just one less thing to worry about."

"Yeah, you're working on that Shakespeare play, right?" Scott asked as someone yelled "Heads up!" He turned and effortlessly caught the ball that was winging right for Faith's head.

Faith stared in amazement. "How do you do that?"

"Reflexes," he told her. "So what is this play

you're working on?"

"*Macbeth,*" Faith told him. "The one with the spots."

"Spots?"

She began rubbing her hands over and over as though she had just put too much cold cream on them. "'Out, damned spot! Out I say! One, two: why, then, 'tis time to do't.'"

Scott applauded with gusto. "You make it look like fun. Too bad you're not one of the actors or I'd actually come to see it."

"Never!" Faith twisted around to sit more comfortably in the crook of his arm. "I stay strictly behind the scenes. I don't have the nerve to get out there and perform. Actually, it's going to take all the nerve I've got to work with the guest director, Lawrence Briscoe."

"Oh, yeah? What's his story?"

"Well, he thinks he's England's royal gift to every girl on campus, and if you don't have what he calls 'a passion for the theater'—read that, a passion for *him*—he can make your life rather difficult."

"Sounds like you've already had a duel with the dude."

Faith felt herself blushing. "I'm really not worried," she told him, and somewhere, deep down, she realized she wasn't. She was making a real effort to make her life less rigid, and it seemed to be working. Going out with Scott was a big part of it. "I'm trying to keep cool about the whole thing. I mean, it's just a play, after all, and he's just a guy who's full of himself. I can handle it."

Scott made a telescope of his hands and sighted down an imaginary barrel at Faith. "You know what?" he said.

"What?"

"We haven't played a game in almost twenty minutes. How about I go reserve the badminton court and you go get the birdies?"

"You're on," Faith said. She quickly got to her feet and, after blowing Scott a kiss, raced off to the equipment box on the far side of the field. Things were going to be all right. They really were. She felt like a bird herself, liberated and free.

"This is a perfect end to the picnic," KC said, sighing. "Look, have you ever seen a more beautiful sunset?" She turned in Peter Dvorsky's arms so that she could read the expresson in his light brown eyes.

"I don't know," Peter said. His eyes weren't on the sky, but on her. "When there's so much beauty around, it's hard to know where to look."

KC smiled. "You're such a flatterer," she said. But she knew Peter always meant what he said. He was direct and honest and the guy KC was crazy about.

"But now that you mention it," Peter murmured in her ear, "I ought to get a camera and do some shooting before we leave. Maybe they don't have sunsets like this in Italy. Anything's possible."

"I still can't believe all this has worked out so perfectly," KC said. "Thank heavens for Grandma Rose."

Peter shifted his weight in the hay so that he was leaning more securely on the side of the wagon, which had just started down the road that led from the main campus out to the fields of the ag school. "We should all have someone with a little extra money who believes in us, just like the artists did in the Renaissance," he declared. Then, lifting an imaginary glass, he toasted, "Here's to your grandma Rose, whose generosity makes it possible for you to go to Florence with me."

"So I can study business while you study photography at Academy of the Arts. Hoorah for Rose!" KC chimed in.

They clinked their fingers together. Then Peter dropped his imaginary glass and drew KC's hand to his mouth for a soft, sweet kiss.

KC wondered at the incredible energy running through her body. This had to be love. There was nothing that could describe this feeling that was both floating and grounded, both fragile and resilient.

The sun had slipped out of sight and the sky was dimming. The smell of the sweet, fragrant hay in the wagon filled her nostrils, and she decided she now knew what it meant to be completely happy.

The wagon pulled hard around a corner and started past the ag school. There was herd of Guernsey cows to their right, some standing up, some lying in the soft grass. KC stared around at the other people in the wagon, most of whom were clustered in twos, either embracing or talking quietly. "Do you think you'll be homesick?" she asked Peter suddenly, thinking of Winnie and Faith, and of her hard-won place in the Tri Beta sorority.

"Me? Well, you know me. I'm a one-contact-sheet man. Besides, I'll have my best model along with me. I mean, yeah, I guess I'll miss a few of my good buddies, and I'm probably going to feel like a real dodo because I can't speak Italian, but I'll just stick close to you. Then I'll feel okay again."

KC wanted to jump up and declare how wonderful she felt, but these feelings were too precious to share. They were hers and Peter's alone.

"Say, would you please remind me to return my library books before we take off?" Peter said. "And those forms for taking a leave of absence."

"You mean you haven't handed them in to the dean of students yet?" She waved a finger in his face.

"Hey, I have enough on my mind with that anthropology test next Saturday. The professor agreed to give it to me early so I can get credit for the course." He ran a hand through his blond hair. "One thing I will not do is get a haircut. I want to start looking Italian."

KC laughed. "Fat chance. You've got those all-American features."

"You'll see, I'm going to eat pasta three times a day when we get there," Peter said, lifting his baggy sweater and pulling at his belt. "My mom always says I'm too skinny. Now's my chance to get a belly."

"I'm going to eat *gelato* constantly," KC said. "I won't even think about fat content. It's supposed to be the best ice cream in the world. They've got it in every flavor, like mint chocolate and almond and macaroon and fish."

"Fish!" Peter yelled. Everyone in the wagon looked up.

"I'm not kidding," KC said. "I read it in that guidebook you gave me. They make *gelato* out of everything—carrots, zucchini, and this gray stuff that's like flounder."

"Gross." Peter made a face. They jolted to a halt suddenly and saw that the horses had stopped by the side of a silo to get a drink of water from the trough. "Just in case we get really homesick, we should get the address of the best American fast food in Florence. You know anyone who's been to Italy?"

KC lost her balance and nearly fell over as the wagon started again. Peter used the opportunity to steady her with an arm around her waist.

KC snuggled against him. "My dad was there, but that was way before fast food. He bummed around Europe in his hippie period after his senior year in college."

"I bet you could hitch rides in those days without thinking you'd get kidnapped or killed," Peter said with a sigh.

KC nodded. "My dad hitched everywhere," she said, suddenly flashing on her father, his thin, bearded face, giving her the I've-been-around-so-let-me-tell-you-how-it-really-is lecture. They'd been washing dishes in the back of the health food restaurant her dad and mom ran, and KC had been complaining about how totally disorganized her father was. She criticized his bookkeeping and told him how she was going to get him on track. And he had looked at her soulfully and said, "Kahia Cayenne, there are things on earth more important than keeping books."

"Did your dad see the Alps?" Peter asked. "I've always wanted to photograph the Alps," he added wistfully.

"I don't know about that. But he hung out with these Moroccan peddlars in Sicily and lived in a tent for two months," KC answered. She had never been close to her father, but for all their differences, she really loved him. Even though he wasn't sure about her decision to take a semester off from U of S and follow Peter, he'd given her his blessing. He'd actually said, "If this guy is important to you, you'll find out there. And if he's not, you'll find out about life, and that's worth everything."

She turned to Peter to tell him, but before she could speak, he had pressed her close and was planting gentle kisses on her cheeks and hair. She closed her eyes and thanked her stars for Peter, her father, and for Grandma Rose. Truly, she had to be the luckiest girl alive.

Four

············

Winnie clunked down the orange-carpeted corridor of Forest Hall on her roller blades, not caring about the racket she was making. So it was midnight. So it was rude of her. It wasn't any worse than those beer cans somebody had left in the hall. She kicked one aside with her skate.

The picnic had been horrible. All she could think about was Josh—or rather her lack of Josh. All the barbecued beef and lemonade in the world wasn't going to solve that problem.

Winnie skidded to a stop in the doorway of her room as she spied a couple of large high-tops under her desk. They belonged to Brooks Baldwin, her roommate Melissa's fiancé, who was parked on Winnie's chair. He had shoved aside her brand-new collection of red bottle tops so that he could work on a hand-held video game.

Winnie glared at him, and then her gaze shifted down to the floor where her roommate, Melissa McDormand, was stretching on the floor in her running shorts.

The room was its typical schizo self—Winnie's half decked out with clothing that had never seen a hanger, posters, magazine clippings, and unusual "found" objects, like the rusty milk can she'd salvaged when she passed a house in Springfield where people were moving out. It made a perfect wastebasket, Winnie thought. The other half of the room—Melissa's half—was neat as a store window, with nothing on the walls and no strewn clothes.

"You two are up late," Winnie commented as she glided into the room. Mel was the early-to-bed, early-to-rise kind who was always under the covers by midnight.

Brooks just nodded at Winnie. "So Mel, do you really think running and medicine are in some way connected?"

"Other than me being a good example to my

patients, sure," Melissa answered. Her coppery red ponytail bounced as she drew her head to her legs and pulled down. "I mean, becoming a physician takes the same kind of discipline as running laps."

Winnie careened into her bed and sat down hard, pulling off one skate. *This* was what nearly married people talked about? If she and Josh ever started sounding like robots communicating over a time-space continuum, that would be the day she'd kill herself. *Where're your emotions, for heaven's sake!* Winnie wanted to yell.

Ever since Melissa and Brooks had gotten engaged, they had been having these marathon gab sessions late into the night. But Winnie hadn't heard them discussing the important topic—their marriage.

"So, you guys just back from the picnic?" Winnie asked.

"No, we really couldn't fit it into our schedule," Brooks told her.

"Right." Winnie pulled off the other skate. Brooks and Melissa were staring at her, making her feel as if the FBI were watching her for suspicious behavior. "Well, nice to see you guys," Winnie said. "But I'm outta here."

She went to her closet for her running shoes and plunked down on the floor to lace them. The air was so thick with robot friction, she could have cut it with a hacksaw. She raced for the door.

"It's midnight," Winnie heard Melissa say. "What are you planning to do?"

"What everyone does at this witchly hour," Winnie said, as she walked out of their dorm room. "Jog."

She hurried down the stairs of Forest Hall and out into the pitch-black night. The air was a little chilly, so Winnie pumped her legs briskly and headed toward the trees on the opposite side of the quad. There wasn't a soul around.

Nothing like a little terror to get the adrenaline going, Winnie assured herself. *I could start a new program for the athletic department: Fitness Through Fear. It might catch on.*

She ran down a hill and jumped over a low hedge that separated the quad from the athletic fields. Running along the back of the gym and around the football stadium, she started on the footpath alongside the tennis courts. The nets flapped gently in the light wind, and Winnie inhaled deeply. It was exciting being out here all by herself, moving through space like she owned it. There was something about running—not just the high she always got—but the complete freedom. When her body and brain were in perfect rhythm, she felt she could do no wrong.

Then she heard it. Her own footfalls sounded absolutely regular, but another set of feet had a different tempo. Someone was running behind her. *Phap, phap, breathe. Phap, phap, breathe.* Each slap on the ground came right after hers.

Despite what she'd told Melissa, it wasn't common to run into other joggers at this time of night. A sudden panic shot through her entire body.

God, Winnie, get out of here, she told herself. This is the nineties for heaven's sake. Night joggers are prime targets.

She ran faster, hoping to blot out the sound of the other runner, but when her speed picked up, so did his. It had to be a him. The footfalls were too heavy for another woman.

Without wanting to, Winnie turned briefly, hoping that the sounds weren't real. Maybe they were just paranoid hallucinations. But as soon as she looked back Winnie spotted a tall man. It was too dark to see features, but she could tell from his shape that he was strong and well built.

She bit her lip and said a small prayer, then really put on the speed.

"Hey, wait up!"

Oh, Mom, Winnie thought. *I'm sorry I had that*

big fight with you when I was thirteen. I mean, you were acting like such a single mother and such a shrink. I had to rebel. And I never did get my nose pierced anyhow, so what was it all about? Then she thought about Josh. Would he miss her? Probably not.

"Come on, slow down. Give me a break."

It was impossible. He was right on her heels. Winnie gave another quick glance over her shoulder and saw that the runner was wearing a U-of-S track suit, the same kind Melissa wore. Did that mean he belonged on campus? The thought made her feel only slightly better.

Then he was by her side, matching his rhythm to hers. "You really like sprinting, don't you?" he asked.

For a second Winnie looked straight ahead, wondering if she could just keep him talking until they got to Greek Row. That would allow her to go pound on the door of the Tri Beta sorority and scream bloody murder until someone woke up. Without breaking pace, she glanced sideways at him. He was grinning.

"I know you from somewhere," he said. "Do I look familiar?" His voice was mellow, hardly affected by the hard running, but Winnie could detect a hint of an accent she couldn't place.

"I don't know you," Winnie said. "Could you leave me alone, please?"

"Wait a second, I'll figure it out."

"Figure what out?" Winnie gasped as she tripped over a crack in the pavement.

"I have total recall. It's not western civ, is it?"

Winnie ran faster.

"And it's not that big poli-sci course. Sure, I can pin you exactly." He reached over and grabbed her wrist. She wheeled around and jerked to a halt beside him just as they made it off campus, onto the Springfield street that led into town. Standing next to him, she suddenly felt very small and terribly weak. She wanted to cry. There wasn't a car or a person in sight. Her knees began to buckle.

"Psych," he said. "The big Tuesday lecture. I saw you once there, and then I spotted you again the day we first went over to the med school for our lab assignments." He let go of her hand but she still felt the pressure where he'd grabbed her.

So he wasn't exactly a stranger. They were both doing scut work for the graduate students at the medical school.

"I noticed you right away," he told her. "You were wearing a pair of jeans with lace-mesh cutouts and a flowered vest about seven sizes too big for you."

"Yeah, that was me," Winnie said. She was breathing hard, but it was more from panic than from exertion. She took a good look at him.

He had short dark hair worn slightly longer in front so that it curled over one eye. But beneath the hair, she could just make out the faint line of a scar across his left eyebrow.

His face wasn't traditionally handsome—the eyes were too close together—but the sum of the features was striking. Winnie also noticed his stillness. He didn't shift his weight around and fidget like most guys she knew. He just stood there, balanced on the balls of his feet, staring into her eyes with complete confidence. She wondered how old he was—he looked a lot more mature than Josh, maybe even older than some seniors.

Then he smiled and held out his hand. "Maybe we should be polite and tell each other our names."

She liked his accent. It was like music when he spoke.

"I guess you're right." She sighed and put her hand in his. "Winnie Gottlieb."

He covered her hand with both of his. "Dimitri Costigan Broder."

Winnie burst into nervous laughter.

"What's funny?"

"Pretty fancy name," she said, shrugging. "I mean, it's a nice name, but it's unusual."

Dimitri smiled, and one deep dimple appeared in his right cheek. "Actually, I was named for my grandfather, who was supposedly some kind of prince back before World War Two. He was killed in a fighter plane. So, royalty being kind of scarce, my mother decided to keep the tradition going."

Winnie scanned Dimitri's face as he spoke. In the dim light, it had a changeable quality to it— sometimes tough, sometimes vulnerable.

She wondered about the scar across his eyebrow. Maybe it was a dueling scar, like in the old days when men used to cross swords over a beautiful woman.

"You're not getting chilled, are you?" Dimitri asked suddenly. He had a serious way of taking her in that unnerved her. "Here, take this." He stripped off his lightweight cotton jacket and draped it around her shoulders. It was amazingly warm from his body heat. "Let's keep moving," he directed her, and then started in at a very slow jog again.

"It's nice to have company. Shall I tell you the story of my life?" he asked with a teasing lilt to his voice.

"If you'd like," Winnie said.

"Well, my father worked for the government and we traveled around a lot when I was a kid."

"That must have been tough," Winnie said, sneaking another glance at him. "It's not easy to make friends when you're always moving."

"No, but I loved it. I'm a born traveler. And we hit some strange places, like Papua, New Guinea, and Madagascar. We were in Nepal for a couple of years." He effortlessly kicked a stone out of her path without ever losing his pace.

Winnie was truly impressed. Her summer in Paris seemed almost dull compared to where he'd been.

"I guess wanderlust is in my blood, because after high school I took a few years off to travel. Kind of needed to experiment a little with life."

That's why he's so much older. Maybe twenty-five, Winnie thought. She slipped her arms through the sleeves of his jacket. The whiff of his after-shave, some fresh herbal scent, made her a little dizzy.

"So what are you doing in dull old Springfield?" Winnie wanted to know.

Dimitri shrugged as they rounded a corner. "I needed a college degree." He tugged on the drawstring of his pants, pulling the waistband tighter over his flat stomach. "I'm interested in politics. I figured if I wanted to be the leader of a nation someday, I need the credentials."

Winnie nodded. "You're a poli-sci major?"

"Yes, but I run at least as much as I study, to keep my head on straight." He leaned closer, and for a brief moment their hands brushed together. "Now that I've talked your ear off, tell me all about you."

Winnie was so startled by the accidental touch, she jerked her fingers away. "Oh, me." She suddenly felt terribly boring. "I come from Jacksonville, a town about two hours away. I enjoy alligator wrestling and ballroom dancing, in that order, and I'm studying the history of cave paintings."

Dimitri stopped running and she did, too, as if magnetically drawn to his lead.

"You are the person I've been looking for," he said, staring into her eyes and taking two steps toward her.

Winnie couldn't move. She felt as if electricity were coursing from her chest down to her feet and up through the top of her head. It wasn't from panic this time—but from exhilaration.

Then Dimitri blinked, and the moment was over. "You always jog in the middle of the night?" he asked curiously.

"Only when I'm feeling restless."

"I know exactly what you mean. Tonight my blood is really pumping. Say, there's that old pioneer graveyard behind the dorm green. Let's jog through there."

Winnie exhaled quickly. Everybody stayed away from that graveyard. "Oh, I don't really—"

"Chicken?"

"Who, me?" He had his nerve. "Of course not. I just never go there anymore, that's all."

"Winnie, Winnie." He trailed one finger around the outline of her face and let it come to rest right on the center of her forehead. "Look through your third eye, see the impossible. Then take the risk." The warmth of his hand spread over her face, as though the sun had touched it.

"The greater the fear, the bigger the thrill," he whispered. He stepped back and stood quietly, waiting for her to make up her mind.

Winnie hesitated for a minute. Now that she was in a safe and steady relationship with Josh, her wild ways had been tamed. But what was wrong with being a little radical? There was safe—and there was dull, which is what she and Josh had become lately. Didn't she want to take life by the throat and shake it up? So why was she standing here like a scaredy-cat? This was her chance to have a different, unusual time with a real soulmate.

"Let's do it. Tag, you're it!" Winnie tapped him

on the back and started running full tilt. Her feet flew over the pavement as she circled around and sped toward the campus again.

Dimitri screamed and took a leap past her.

"Me first! MOVE ASIDE!" Winnie shouted, overtaking him. Her feet barely skimmed the earth as they rounded the dorm green. She could see the cemetery ahead, and whether it was in her imagination or not, she suddenly felt a blast of cold air coming from the dark beyond her. Her breath caught in her throat.

She slowed down and felt the whoosh of Dimitri passing her as he neatly hurdled over the small stone fence that divided the campus from the cemetery. Her legs shaking, Winnie came up behind him slowly and let herself in through the rusted double gates.

The main path was thickly overgrown, so Winnie really had to lift her feet. A gnarled tree root made her stumble, and she gasped, almost imagining that a ghostly hand had reached out and grabbed her ankle. She sprinted to catch up with Dimitri, who was plowing ahead as though he were running on a track. He was like an animal in the dark, she thought, totally sure of his footing and his place.

"Yowee!" Dimitri yelled as she came up beside

him. Winnie gave a war whoop of her own, and Dimitri answered it. The two of them howled like wolves, shattering the peace of the graveyard. They were trying to outshout each other, and Winnie was getting so hoarse she started laughing and so did he. They were too hysterical to run anymore, and Winnie gave up first, collapsing in a heap.

She stopped laughing when she rolled over and saw that she had almost landed on a flat tombstone. "This is creepy," she said with a shiver. "Maybe we should rejoin the living."

But before she had a chance to get up, Dimitri threw himself down beside her. With tears of laughter running down his cheeks, he grabbed her and hugged her.

Winnie felt his arms tighten around her. It felt wonderful and exciting and passionate, but just as she was beginning to melt into the swoony moment she saw Josh's face. *Oh, jeez, Winnie, watch yourself! This is fabulous, but you're not exactly available. You're attached to Josh.*

She put her hands up to Dimitri's chest as a barricade. "I can't do this after running. Gives me a stitch in my side," she joked.

"Okay. No sweat." He held out a hand and she took it. "It's been a swell evening."

"Yes, it has," she said, and meant it. "I guess I'll be going back to my dorm now."

"I'll jog you there."

"No, that's okay. I'll be fine," Winnie said, not wanting to take the chance that Josh might be waiting up for her in the dorm lobby.

"All right. My dorm's over that way." Dimitri pointed through the trees. "So, I'll say good night and I guess I'll be seeing you in the med-school lab. Tuesday, four P.M., right?"

"See you then." She nodded, handing back his jacket.

He slipped it on and bent down close to her ear. "I like your style," he said. Then he sprinted off, through the tombstones.

Winnie watched him for a moment, trying to calm down. But it was useless. All her circuits were firing, one right after the other. Then she took off down the same path, racing for all she was worth. She didn't know if she was going this fast because she wanted to get away from the tombstones and overhanging dead branches, or because she had to get out all the bubbly feelings Dimitri had churned up in her.

When she got back to Forest Hall, one fluorescent light was still on in the lounge, right over the Ping-Pong table. The soda machine hummed softly.

Panting for breath, she walked further into the room and realized sounds were coming from the TV.

Josh had crashed in one of the big easy chairs. His bare feet were curled up under him and the hand that wore the woven bracelet supported his neck at an odd angle. He sighed in his sleep and muttered, "Love you, Win."

Winnie gazed down at him, and all the excitement she'd felt in the graveyard seemed to drain out of her. What could she have been thinking of, going to the graveyard with that strange guy? She suddenly felt very tender. "You kept our TV date," she murmured.

But what good did it do for him to be there if he couldn't even stay up to see her? "Oh, you're such a . . . I don't know what," she muttered, getting angry with him all over again.

"Hey, you, rise and shine," she said, picking up one of his limp hands and patting his cheek with it.

"What? Who's it?" Josh blinked and rubbed one eye, which opened slowly to take in Winnie.

"Josh, what have you got against going to bed?" she demanded, yanking him up and steering him down the hall. "That's where the best sleeping takes place, you know."

"Uh-huh. Okay." He allowed himself to be led

to his room, where she opened the door for him and pushed him inside with a quick good night.

As for her, she probably wouldn't be able to sleep.

Five

....

Brooks knew he had to talk to Melissa about their wedding. They were supposed to be studying on the dorm green, but Brooks couldn't concentrate, couldn't study, couldn't remember a thing he'd read. He shifted his weight from his right elbow to his left and glanced at Melissa. "Want to tackle that calculus problem?" he suggested.

"Hmm?"

Melissa was buried in her chemistry textbook, oblivious to him as well as to the study group beside them doing a conversational-French drill.

Brooks cleared his throat. "Let's help each other

out, Melissa. Honors college students have to stick together."

No reaction.

Is this what it's going to be like when we're married? he thought suddenly. *Silence and small talk, figuring out the bills, marching through life putting one foot ahead of the other?*

Getting through that awful meal with their parents when they'd announced their engagement had been bad enough. The tension at that dinner table was so thick you could have spread it on bread. The closemouthed McDormands versus the gabby Baldwins. Practially no talk about their wedding. And ever since that night, neither Brooks nor Melissa had so much as mentioned it.

But when were they going to get around to it? Brooks knew brides-to-be usually talked nonstop about wedding gowns and veils, and whether to leave china swans wearing tutus as favors at each table, or little net bags full of foul-tasting candy inside. But Melissa didn't talk about these or any other nuptial-related things.

When were they even going to set a date? Lately, they'd been talking about homework, dorm food, the track team, mountain climbing—absolutely everything but getting married. Brooks almost had the impression they'd never gotten engaged. He half expected Melissa to look at him and say, "You? Do I know *you*?"

Melissa closed her chem book and started to open her biology-lab notes. Brooks jammed his hand between the pages. "Melissa!" he practically yelled.

She blinked. "I wish you wouldn't interrupt me when I'm studying," she said in a low, firm voice.

"Mel, I'm sorry, but I have an important question to ask you."

"Okay, shoot. What is it?"

"Ah. It's . . . the spring formal. We haven't really talked about it."

"Do we have to talk? I just assumed we were going." She fumbled in her purse for her watch. "Oh, no. It's two-thirty. I have track practice at three."

"Relax, Mel. You've got plenty of time," Brooks said, berating himself for not mentioning what was really on his mind. But the next words out of his mouth did not touch on the subject either. "Tell me, how's Winnie?" he blurted out.

Melissa looked up at him. "Winnie? Okay, I guess. She's been putting in a lot of time at the med-school lab with her mice for the last few days." She pulled the elastic from her ponytail, flopped her head over between her knees, smoothed the hair into her hands, and replaced the elastic, then started collecting her books. "I guess I'll see you later. I want to warm up really well today before I run."

Brooks's head was pounding. He stood up, feeling slightly light-headed with anger.

"Melissa, I don't really care about Winnie's mice. I care about you and me," he said quickly. "We're going to be married! We've just been through a fairly weird meeting with our parents because of this decision—a decision we made, together."

Mel looked at her shoes, then over at the trees.

Brooks started to pace. "Why aren't we figuring out what's going on here? You and I are not communicating. Doesn't that bother you?"

Melissa barely reacted. There was a faraway look on her face.

But Brooks refused to give up. This was too important. "Are you worried about our honors college revie this week—is that it?"

Melissa reached over and retied her shoelace.

Jeez, this was hard for him to do. The idea of making a commitment that would last his whole life was terrifying—but he'd made it and he thought she had, too. These days, though, it looked like she'd rather think about molecules than marriage.

"Look, I'm jumpy about school, too," Brooks

confessed. "I hate sitting down for my monthly progress report with Professor Sheehy. So is that your problem, Melissa? Nerves?" His blue eyes were begging for a real response.

"No, my grades are pretty good. I'm not worried," Melissa said softly.

"Then what *is* it?" Brooks asked, bending down next to her. "We're supposed to be planning a wedding. We're supposed to be getting closer to each other, not farther away."

Melissa bit her lip and nodded, but wouldn't look at him.

"You know, when we had dinner with our folks, I could see how hard it was for you," Brooks said. "My parents came with presents and were all excited for us. Your parents didn't shower us with gifts or congratulations and they didn't even seem to be all that happy."

Melissa got to her feet so quickly that she knocked Brooks over backward. "*I'm* not the one with the problem, Brooks. *You* are. Your family does everything for you, don't they? Well, mine never had any money, like yours did. That doesn't give you the right to look down your noses at us."

"What are you talking about?"

"Don't play innocent with me," Melissa warned him.

"When my folks walked into the reception room in their old, drabby clothes, I saw you looking through them. You were embarrassed."

"Melissa! You're twisting everything—"

"Am I? Well, maybe you don't think my family's good enough for you! Maybe—" Her voice broke, so she started again. "Maybe you don't think I'm good enough for *you* either. Well, you're not stuck. You don't have to go through with the marriage plans just because you made a promise and you're the kind of person who never breaks promises. Don't do *me* any favors."

She grabbed her books, pens and papers spilling around her. Quickly, she shoved them inside her bag and stalked away across the green.

Brooks had never felt so alone. Or so lonely.

Faith put her books down in one of the burgundy velour seats in the back row of the University Theater. She didn't know what was going to happen between her and Lawrence Briscoe, but she was ready for anything he had to dish out. After all, this was the new Faith, the easygoing, take-life-as-it-comes drama major.

The houselights were up, and she could see Briscoe in the middle of the theater deep in conference with Merideth Paxton, the stage manager. Faith saw them both look up when she walked in, so she knew she'd been noticed.

"All right!" Merideth yelled, looking over his wire-rim glasses. "Act Three, Scene Five. People, listen up! I need the witches and Hecate onstage pronto."

The other crew members were milling around the stage, testing out the setpiece trees. Several actors were running through lines in the corner. Faith wondered what her assignment would be. She craved some really good job on this show.

"Guess who?" said a distinctive brassy voice from behind her. At the same time a pair of hands clapped down over her eyes.

"The Bride of Frankenstein," Faith answered.

"Nope." Liza Ruff removed her hands and whirled Faith around to face her. "'Tis I, Third Witch. How could you miss it—there's no one else like me!"

Boy, is that ever true, Faith thought with a sigh. *There's no one as obnoxious as my roommate.*

Liza was decked out in a huge black cape with a hood that covered her masses of red curls. Her face was plastered with clown white and she was spilling out of a tight black leotard. Her huge eyes were rimmed with liner and too much black mascara. She had put a large putty wart right on the end of her nose. In four words, she was a sight.

"Whad'ya think? Am I witchy enough?" Liza asked.

Faith lowered her eyes, taking in Liza's spangled white boots. "I've never exactly imagined Shakespeare done like you'll do it," she said with a wry smile.

Liza brayed with laughter, and several people standing nearby looked over at them. "Hey, I'll give the old Bard a run for his money," Liza said. "Thank heavens Larry saw the character the way I did."

Faith smirked. So it was "Larry," was it? Liza, like Faith, had been invited to Lawrence Briscoe's den for a private audition. But after Faith insisted that the meeting was not to exploit her talent but her body, Liza had wisely decided not to show up for her date. She realized that it meant giving up a shot at Lady Macbeth, but that didn't bother Liza too much. She still felt that any part on any stage was better than none.

They both looked up as Merideth whistled between his teeth to get everyone's attention for the start of rehearsal.

Faith glanced over at Lawrence Briscoe, who raised his bristling eyebrows and one finger in her direction. Was that a summons to the throne?

Maybe the great man had actually thought of something for her to do.

Faith straightened the bib on her light blue overalls and walked down the raked aisle toward him. "Yes, Mr. Briscoe?"

"Faith, I would so desperately love a cup of tea," the director said in a British accent that sounded absurdly exaggerated. "Do you think you could manage that, dear?"

Faith licked her lips and counted to ten. Dealing with Lawrence Briscoe was like handling a boa constrictor. He was fine until you crossed him, and then he'd squeeze the life out of you, after he'd bitten you.

"I'll get the tea," Faith said, "but I wonder whether I could be assigned something a little more challenging, like props or—"

"Props! Well, that takes a certain creative bent," Briscoe said, rubbing the bridge of his long nose. "A passion for discovery and exploration. You're a rather prim and proper girl, you know. Uptight, isn't that the American term? I simply don't find that passion for the theater in you."

You mean you don't find a willing victim who's ready to meet you in a dark corner for some lechy groping, Faith thought. How dare he!

"I've always thought that some of the greatest

backstage work is done by those with organized minds," she said as calmly as she could. "People who have a great sense of responsibility. Why look at Meredith. He's organized and detail-oriented, qualities that make him a super stage manager."

"Meredith is a young man, my dear," Briscoe said, blatantly looking her up and down. "Those are admirable qualities in a man. In a woman, however, we look for something . . . something more unusual."

"I am unusual!" Faith blurted out. "Just try giving me something to do and I'll prove it to you."

"You have your nerve," he said, smiling, even though his eyes were cold and accusatory. "You owe me quite a lot."

Faith felt a nervous pang in her stomach as she remembered her debt. Briscoe had in fact come to her rescue when she was on probation for buying beer with a fake ID. Faith had been trying to ditch a bottle of champagne Brooks Baldwin's parents had brought for Brooks and Melissa's engagement dinner, when Erin Grant, her tyrannical resident adviser at Coleridge Hall had run right into her. If Briscoe hadn't snatched the champagne, telling Erin Grant it was a stage prop, Erin would have reported Faith for breaking probation. Faith would have gotten kicked right out of school.

Of course Briscoe was no angel. He hadn't helped Faith because he was a nice guy. He clearly expected to get something in return.

Faith hated him. He was smug and repulsive, and in just a few years, his high forehead would be a receding hairline. He'd be nearly bald by the time he was thirty-five.

However, he was in charge of this production and she had decided that if groveling was the way to go, then grovel she would. "It was very kind of you to help me," she said between clenched teeth.

A huge clatter of metal caused them to turn their attention to the back of the house.

"What is all that noise?" Briscoe demanded. "Meredith! What are you doing back there?"

Meredith was standing with his hands on his hips, yelling at a willowy brunette with a pair of Raybans stuck on her head. Two large brass torches lay at her feet where she'd dropped them. Her straight hair was pulled tight in a chignon at the nape of her neck, making her thin, elongated face seem gaunt.

Faith frowned at the sight of Erin Grant, Lady MacBeth in the flesh. And Faith knew just how she'd won the leading part, too. By cozying up to Lawrence Briscoe on her call back date.

"Erin just made her entrance, Mr. Briscoe,"

Meredith explained. "Twenty minutes late to rehearsal. I'm docking her."

"Now, now, let's not be hasty," Briscoe said. "I told Erin to arrive a bit late today. How are you, my dear?"

Erin gave him a saccharine smile. "Never better, Larry." Then she turned her frosty blue eyes on Faith. "You're the go-fer, aren't you?"

Faith bristled. "I'm on the crew," she corrected her.

"Uh-huh. Well, I'm parched. I wonder if you'd run down to the snack machines and get me some red grape juice. The organic brand, you know, the one I always drink." She reached into her red leather clutch and produced a dollar, which she shoved at Faith.

"And don't forget the tea, Faith," Briscoe added, putting an arm around Erin's thin shoulders and leading her away. "Now," Faith heard him say to her, "let's discuss your character a bit while Meredith runs through the witches and Hecate."

Faith barged through the open doors of the theater and ran through the lobby to the staircase. She took the stairs two at a time and rammed her hip against the green-room door so hard, she knew there'd be a huge bruise there that evening. Oh, why was she letting Erin and Briscoe get to her?

She went to the table beside the snack machine and snatched up a tea bag, pouring boiling water over it into a cup for Briscoe.

Erin was a bitch, but Faith had to be nice to her or risk more citations. And if Lawrence was such a petty monster that he needed to torture her as revenge for her rejecting him, well, Faith could handle it. The important thing was the show. She'd just ignore their rotten behavior and act like a pro. Maybe it would inspire Lawrence and Erin to be a little more professional, too.

She fed the dollar into the machine and pressed the juice button. The can came rolling out. She thought about taking a straw, but decided she'd enjoy watching Erin have to gulp the stuff out of the can top.

Walking carefully up the stairs with the hot tea in one hand and the juice can in the other, Faith pretended she was a princess disguised as the serving girl in some kid's story. Heroines always got rid of the bad guys, in fairy tales.

The houselights had been turned halfway down, and there was a hush in the theater. Faith inched her way down the partly darkened aisle until she saw Briscoe standing to one side. She slid up behind him. "Here's your tea."

He turned abruptly. "Quiet as a mouse, aren't

you?" he said, letting his fingers graze hers as he took the steaming cup. "Such cold hands," he said. "I know what would warm them up."

Faith wondered if she was going to spend the entire four weeks of rehearsal dodging his bullets. "My thermostat's fine," she said. She looked up as Liza gave a terrible cackle onstage.

There was a disgusted grunt from the row ahead of them. "Oh, I can't concentrate at all," Erin complained. "Lawrence!" She got out of her seat and flounced up to Briscoe, giving Faith a jealous glare. "They're making such a racket up there. How can I possibly—oh, you got my juice." She whipped the can out of Faith's hand and popped the top without aiming it away. A spray of deep red sparkled for a second in the air before landing on the bib of Faith's light blue overalls.

"Oh, Faith, why are you always underfoot!" Erin ranted on.

Faith tried hard not to scream, even though she knew grape-juice stains seldom come out. Slowly, catching her breath, she drew a tissue from her back pocket and blotted the purple liquid.

Meredith came racing up the aisle with Liza at his heels. "We're exploring the witches' pagan feelings, Mr. Briscoe."

Liza nodded. "Really, Larry, don't worry about

how it sounds now. We'll tone down the volume as we get closer to performance."

"Everyone around here is inept," Erin shrieked, but her comment was directed at Faith.

Faith could feel Meredith staring at her in sympathy. Then he looked down at her overalls. "Faith," he said quietly, "listen, don't feel bad. I've got a great job for you."

Faith swallowed hard, taking comfort in knowing that Winnie would have a way to fix this—like tie-dyeing the overalls with more grape juice.

"I'm okay," Faith said. "It's not as bad as it looks."

Briscoe cleared his throat. "Well, I'm glad to hear that. I certainly don't intend to allow the entire rehearsal to fall apart because of some minor incident. Meredith, protecting your little friend from her recent tragedy is awfully gallant of you, but if she's not mature enough to handle something so minuscule by herself, we don't really want her on the crew, do we? No use crying over spilled juice, eh?" He strode majestically toward the stage.

Erin, with an I-told-you-he'd-want-you-to-get-lost look at Faith, followed him down the aisle.

Liza shook her head at her roommate. "Looks like you better shape up, Faith. You're not so indispensible." Then with a flourish of her cape, Liza walked away.

Faith was seething. She wanted to stick with her carefree, hang-loose attitude, but everything was falling apart. First, stupid Max had gone off with her wonderful leather book bag. Then Scott had warned her that he might not be around for Spring Formal. Now her new overalls were ruined.

What an awful day. She couldn't decide whom she hated more—Erin, Briscoe, or Liza the witch.

Six

"KC, snap out of it," Winnie directed.

"What? Oh. I was just thinking," KC said absentmindedly as she, Winnie, and Courtney Conner, the Tri Beta president, walked across the fog-covered campus on Wednesday morning.

"You were mooning."

"Mooning?"

"Yeah, over Peter. I can tell. You might as well be on a lunar probe the way you have that look in your eye."

KC laughed. It was true. She had been thinking about Peter. Her and Peter. Italy and Peter. Always Peter.

"I guess I am a little distracted lately," she admitted. She was going over to the Tri Beta house with Courtney to help decorate the place for her own farewell dinner.

"We'll finish up the bows for the ends of the tables," Courtney said to KC, ignoring Winnie's observations. "Then we'll hang the balloons and streamers. You can vanish for a while so we can set up a few . . . surprises."

KC nodded.

"Boy, you guys sure work hard for a meal," Winnie joked. She gathered her see-through plastic raincoat closer around her and pulled at her hair, trying to get the spikes to stick up despite the wet weather.

"Winnie, we really want to make KC's farewell wonderful, so it should look wonderful, too," Courtney explained.

"I get it. Image counts, right?" Winnie nudged KC. "So you'll be happy to hear that I'm working on my image for Spring Formal. I'm thinking of wearing a conservative tuxedo. Now, Faith's image I'm not so sure about. If she goes, she'll probably wear Liza's scalp on her belt. Boy, is she in a mood!"

Courtney winced. "How gruesome," she said.

"Sorry. When something comes into my mind, it

usually comes out through my mouth. Doesn't it, KC?" Winnie asked.

KC hesitated. She never quite knew what to say around Courtney and Winnie. It was almost as if her two friends spoke different languages. But before she could open her mouth, a car pulled out in front of them and KC felt Courtney jerk her back toward the curb. "KC," Courtney exclaimed. "Please be careful!"

Winnie laughed. "Our friend is physically present, but nowhere mentally to be found. A severe case of Peter Dvorsky."

KC blushed. "Soon, I won't be around for you to tease," she said.

"We're really going to miss you, you know," Courtney told her as she linked her arm through KC's. They were just passing the medical arts building, about two blocks from the University Hospital.

"And I'll miss you," KC said. "All of you," she added.

Winnie sighed. "I've decided to recruit a new friend to stand in for you."

"Who could replace KC?" Courtney demanded.

"His name is Mickey. He's tiny and covered with gray fur. He's not as ambitious as you, KC, and certainly not as pretty, but on the other hand, he has no plans for Europe. In fact he likes being in his cage." Winnie leaped over to the grillwork fence that rimmed the hospital and stuck one foot between the spokes. "Which may be one reason why he appeals to me, since I've been feeling like my life is kind of like a cage lately, too."

KC again didn't know what to say, so she pointed to the hazy halo of mist that surrounded the majestic mountains that ringed Springfield. "I hope Peter took photos. It reminds me of those Italian paintings with cherubs and goddesses."

"Just like the ones you and Peter are going to see when you get to Florence," Courteny said.

KC got a faraway look. "Yeah," she whispered.

"Earth to KC, come in!" Winnie said loudly. "We're about to pass the hospital. Shoud we get you on an EEG machine and jog your brain cells?"

KC grinned a little and linked arms with Winnie. "Sorry. I was thinking of something else." Her gaze drifted across the street as a flash of color caught her eye. She blinked and looked again, stopping in the middle of the intersection.

It couldn't be. But it was. There, at the hospital door, was a familiar figure. How was it possible? Nobody else looked like KC's grandma Rose. She was a tall woman in her midsixties who always wore a hat. She had big picture hats with bunches of cherries and little cute caps with feathers. She'd always told KC it gave her an air of mystery. There she was, wearing a straw boater with a bright pink hatband.

But Grandma Rose lived two hours away in Jacksonville. What on earth would she be doing here? She'd never mentioned that she was coming to Springfield. And with KC about to leave for Italy in just a week, she would definitely have called if she were coming—especially since KC was her favorite granddaughter and she'd just given her this incredibly generous gift so that she could go to Europe.

Suddenly KC started running toward the hospital door.

"What's the matter, KC?" Courtney asked, racing after her.

"Did you see that woman who just went inside?"

"Which one?"

They'd reached the door and KC stepped on the mat that triggered the automatic opening. "She was tall, with a straw hat," KC said. "She looked exactly like my grandma Rose. I must be seeing things. But still, I could swear . . ."

Winnie gave her a disbelieving look. "Listen, I gotta get over to the labs and find little Mickey. He hates it when I'm late. Take it easy, KC. It's probably not your eyesight, just your totally weird-ed-out brain. It'll pass. See you later."

Winnie sprinted off, leaving KC and Courtney standing on the mat. The front door of the hospital stayed open.

"Are you coming with me?" KC asked desperately.

"But you just said it couldn't be your grandmother." Courtney looked at her, puzzled.

"It couldn't be. But I want to check it out anyhow. Please, Courtney." For the first time in a long while, KC realized, she hadn't thought about Peter first.

Courtney smiled and nodded. "The decorations can wait a bit, I guess. The other girls will get started without us. C'mon, let's play detective."

KC raced through the doors. She knew it wasn't Rose. But she had to be sure.

"This is not fun," Winnie groaned. "This is not like high school. This is not life at it's most carefree."

Winnie wrote her name and the time on the sign-in sheet at the lab and opened the door to the mouse room. She'd joked with Courtney and KC about life in a cage, but now that she was at the lab, things were depressing. She couldn't believe she'd missed her chance with Josh again. That morning she'd run into him on her way to the shower. But she'd been so bleary, she'd barely been able to get out a hi.

Later, she'd looked for him at the library and then at the computer center. No luck. That's when she'd run into KC and Courtney and decided to walk off campus with them and check on her mice. To be totally honest with herself, she didn't love the little furry creatures all that much, which meant there was an ulterior motive for going. And the motive had a name—Dimitri.

Dimitri hadn't shown up at the lab yesterday, but so what? Dumb of her not to think that schedules might change or that he got hung up somewhere.

Still, she felt guilty about all the time she'd spent poking around the labs, guilty that she wanted to see somebody other than Josh, and guilty that waiting for Dimitri to show up had caused her to miss her hotline job. She'd started counseling teenagers on the Crisis Hotline not only to make them feel better but to help herself, too. But since she'd met Dimitri, she didn't feel capable of helping anyone—*least* of all, herself.

No Josh. No Dimitri. Okay, just start work and stop thinking about these two guys. After all, this isn't *high school anymore, Win. You're supposed to be a little more grown up!*

Winnie walked down the row of cages, sniffing the air in imitation of the little mice who were milling around, sleeping, eating, exercising, or standing on top of one another. None of them had floppy dark hair, or an accent, or a scar through their left eyebrow, but luckily Winnie had a good imagination.

"Hi, gang!" She waved, then moonwalked over to the food bins. She took a big scoop of pellets and started down the row, distributing a small amount in the slot in the first cage. "And she tried the big bowl of porridge, but it was *too hot,*" Winnie crooned to the bunch of white mice. She measured out a helping that was twice as large as the first and deposited it in the container of the second cage. "So she tried the next bowl, but it was *too cold.*"

She went to the third cage and dumped the remainder of the scoop—a huge portion—into the food slot. "And then she finally tried the last bowl—"

"—and it was *just right,*" said a low voice in her ear.

Winnie felt a pair of hands on her waist, pulling her away from the cage.

"I came in through the back door. I've been watching you," the voice said.

Winnie turned and giggled. Dimitri looked so wonderful in a leather vest worn over a black T-shirt with the sleeves rolled high. He was wearing baggy black silk pants and open rope-soled shoes she'd never seen in American stores. Winnie guessed he'd bought them in Europe, along with the rest of his continental attire.

"So what did you see when you watched me?" Winnie asked.

"The end of freedom," Dimitri answered, wrinkling his forehead.

Winnie gave a nervous laugh. "What does that mean?"

He shook his head sadly. "Winnie, Winnie, don't you see you're as trapped as these poor creatures are by the system? You can't be free until they are."

"Oh, really!"

Dimitri swept his arm along the row of cages. "Does it make you feel powerful to give the animals pleasure or pain?"

"I don't give them any pain," Winnie protested, half smiling because she liked being teased.

"You do! To a mouse, not eating is pain." Dimitri gestured toward the cages with a wave of his arm. "Look at them! See how they're scrambling for scraps."

Dimitri approached the first cage and lifted his index finger over one mouse's nose. He drew a circle in the air. The mouse, as though hypnotized, followed Dimitri's lead. "He wants something, doesn't he? In a minute he'll start gnawing on another fellow victim!"

"But the experiment is about rations," Winnie said, taking her scoop off the top of the cage and starting back to the feed bin for more. "One group gets one ration, the next two, and the next three. And then you get all this data about how they function on less and more food."

"You are a cruel woman," Dimitri growled, standing in her way. When she moved to the right, he moved. When she dodged left, he was there before her. "Grant freedom to this mouse!" he shouted, pointing to one small white creature cowering in the back of the first cage.

Winnie laughed. "You're crazy!" she said, ducking under his arm and moving past him.

He grabbed her. Once again, an electric jolt shot through her, just as it had when they touched in the cemetery.

"Crazy is what it's all about," he whispered. "If you're not crazy, you're boring. Or bored."

Winnie looked straight into his eyes, and the challenge she saw in them took her breath away. "But my psych professor said—" she began desperately.

He put a finger on her lips. "Another authority figure! See what I mean, Win?" Dimitri demanded. "You're in a cage of your own making. Let me set you free!"

Winnie pushed his hand away and started laughing as he took the scoop from her and dumped the entire contents over her head. She was giggling wildly when the door to the lab swung open and a grad student wearing a white coat and a pencil pack in his pocket stuck his head in.

"You two are about a hundred decibels too loud," he complained, shoving his thick glasses up to the bridge of his nose. "And what's all that food doing on the floor?"

Winnie wondered if he always looked like a mole or only when he wrinkled up his nose that way. "Sorry," she said, barely stiffling another set of giggles. "We'll try to be quiet. And we'll clean up."

"Don't try, just do it. What're your names anyway?"

"She is Margaret Fredonia, and I'm Edgar Harp," Dimitri told him seriously. The student scribbled the names in a small black notebook he took from his pocket.

"Another disruption and I'll have to report you," he told them.

When they were alone again, Winnie exploded. "You are terrible!" she yelled. "Who *are* you?"

Dimitri got down on one knee and bowed his head. "I am the man of your dreams. Come with me and I will fill you full of excitement."

"I'll bet," Winnie said, wishing that she could stop comparing him with Josh. She also wished she could stop feeling so confused. "I don't get it," she finally blurted out. "If you're such an exciting guy and I'm so boring, why are you so interested in me?"

"Ah." He leaped up and took her hands in his. "Because I see incredible potential. Any girl who goes running at midnight is a prime candidate for fun. We have so much in common, Winnie. Let me prove it to you by taking you to dinner Friday night."

Dimitri brushed her hand with his lips. His burning bright eyes under long, dark lashes had her spellbound. But suddenly she recalled that Josh had long lashes, too. The spell was broken.

Winnie, how many times do you have to make the same mistake? she thought. She remembered all too well how she'd tried to be involved with two guys at the same time. One was Josh, of course. And the other was Travis, the guy she'd met in Paris the summer before her freshman year. Travis had actually come to Springfield to see her. It was romantic and a little nutsy—but she'd almost lost Josh by being so irresponsible about their relationship. She couldn't do that again.

"No, I really don't think . . ." Winnie said as a picture of Josh formed in her mind. He was sitting at his computer—the computer that was coming between them. Still, she and Josh were a couple. What they had together was strong and real.

"Got a date? Break it," Dimitri said.

On the other hand, Dimitri made her feel more alive than she'd felt in weeks. Months. He was like a forest fire raging inside her.

"Look, I'll let you know," Winnie said. When Dimitri gave her a disappointed frown, she added, "I'll see what I can do."

"Good. Now I better get going on my own project." Dimitri reached into his back pocket and took out a computer printout, which he began to tear into little pieces. "Project completed. I'm onto something else." He tipped an imaginary hat to her and left as he had come, by the lab's backdoor.

Winnie gathered her things quickly and signed

out. She had to speak to Josh, had to get some of the confusion out of her head. She rang for the elevator, but was too impatient to wait, so she hurried to the exit door and flew down the three flights of stairs. She made it to the phones in the lobby and reached into her bag for some change.

She dialed with stiff fingers and waited. Josh's phone rang once, twice, three times, four times.

"Hello." His voice was vague and distant.

"Hi, Josh, it's me. Say, what are we doing Friday night?" Winnie asked, trying to make the words sound lighthearted. Maybe he'd have some terrific mushy notion about spending the evening watching the moon come up over Mill Pond. Whatever he suggested would protect her from herself—and from agreeing to go out with Dimitri.

"Friday? I don't know, Winnie. Look, I'm really humming on my deadline right now. Professor Ransom's going to flip over this project. I'm right in the middle of—"

"You always are. That's what's great about you, Josh. You're never just starting or finishing. You keep to the middle."

There was a moment's silence. "What's wrong, Win?"

"I'm just trying to motivate you to be interested in something other than your computer," Winnie said. "There's a big world out there, Josh, and it's passing you by. So how about it?"

"Yeah, yeah. You're absolutely right. I'm sorry. I really want to see you. Why don't I knock on your door later?"

"How much later?"

"I don't know, but I'll try to—"

"Josh, I hate it when I can't get you to tell me anything directly. I can't stand it when you break our dates." She was steaming, hopping from one foot to the other in the little phone booth. Her quarter dropped down and the operator's dry monotone interrupted to say that she would soon have to deposit more coins in the slot.

There was a pause at the other end of the line. "I have to finish this, Win," Josh finally said. "My whole college career could depend on it. What am I supposed to do?"

She wanted to tell him to get them back to that magical time when they had first fallen in love— to the time when they were inseparable. But she couldn't say that. So she hit him with the big one.

"What you can do is tell me if we're going to Spring Formal or if you have a date with that computer on Saturday night, too." She was so desperate, it didn't even matter to her that she'd totally blown her cool. Life was too short to let the vital questions stay locked up.

Josh exhaled, and when he spoke, he was very calm. "Things take as long as they take, Win. I can't give you a better answer than that. I would love to take you to Spring Formal. Or at least I would've loved it until this phone call, which is really making me kind of crazy, if you want to know."

"Well, you're making me more than crazy, so I guess we're even," she whispered, hardly able to breathe now.

"Yeah. Well, let's talk about it tonight," he said in a gentler voice. "We'll work it out."

"Uh-huh." She couldn't say good-bye—it seemed so final—so she just held on to the phone until she heard it click off at his end.

She put down the receiver and laid her forehead against the cool glass pane of the box. Then she closed her eyes to hold back the tears. A tap on the glass made her remember that this was a public phone and other people were waiting to use it.

But when her eyes flew open, she saw Dimitri standing in front of her. He dangled a small white furry creature by the tail.

"What the . . . Where did you get that mouse?" She opened the folding door and leaned against it, dumbfounded.

"Where do you think? I liberated him from our lab. He's eternally grateful."

Winnie felt so totally paranoid, she had to make herself stop looking up and down the hall as if the cops had been notified and were on their way. "Wait till that grad student catches you," she warned Dimitri. "You are going to get in so much trouble. He'll kill you!"

"Not me. I'm clean." He took her hand in his and deposited the squirming mouse right in her palm, closing her fingers gently around the tiny body. Then he turned around and started sprinting for the door.

"Dimitri!"

"This is your fate. Live with it," he yelled from down the hall. "Meet me at the Blue Whale Restaurant Friday, eight P.M. Look magnificent and don't be late. I'll be waiting."

Then he was gone.

Winnie stood there for a minute, feeling her heart race. Suddenly she became aware that there were two pulses going—one a lot faster than her own. She looked down at her closed hand.

"Oh, Mickey, or whoever you are, what am I going to do about him? And what do I do with you?" She cuddled the mouse close and walked quickly to the front door of the building.

Outside, the late-afternoon sun speckled the grass with patches of warm light. Winnie stooped and opened her hand. The mouse darted away.

"Freedom," she murmured, "to do exactly what you want when you want. Wow, what a concept."

She watched the mouse run until he disappeared under some bushes. Then she walked slowly back toward the campus.

Seven

....

*L*auren's job at the Inn left her dead tired and this Thursday night was no exception. She collapsed on the beat-up couch in her tiny apartment as soon as she walked in the door. Putting her feet up on the fruit crate she used as a coffee table, she rubbed her eyes and grabbed Dash's *His* piece. She'd read the last paragraph about twelve times since last night, but she wanted to read it again:

> *It's the way men and women talk that splits them apart. Miscommunication happens constantly, sort of like a collision of particles in*

*space. Words hit words and explode with mean-
ing. And the meanings that men and women
attach to key concepts, like "love," "sharing,"
"commitment," and "let's go out for a pizza,"
are totally different.*

There was a knock on her door, but Lauren
didn't budge. She already knew who it was and
had no intention of opening up. She stayed put,
reading the paragraph once again.

"Hey!" yelled the voice outside her door. "Look, I
know you're in there. Miss Smith or Smythe or whatever you call yourself, we gotta talk about the rent!"

Her landlord, a huge bear of a man named Jim
Calvin, started pounding on the door. His grandmother, who lived downstairs, had told Lauren
that he was coming over. They weren't going to
let her live there out of the kindness of their
hearts, Mrs. Calvin had snarled at her. As if either
of them had a heart!

Lauren lay down flat on the uncomfortable sofa,
staring up at the naked light bulb in the ceiling
above her. She tried to make herself as small and
silent as possible.

"You owe me two hundred and twenty-five
bucks for last month," Jim yelled. "Rent's due on
the first, no exceptions. It's the twentieth, in case

you don't have a calendar, Miss College Girl."

Lauren shut her eyes and blocked out the landlord's ravings by thinking about Dash's words—and meanings. It sounded like Dash was telling her in his own cool way that their breakup had been a miscommunication. And just like space particles hitting each other and bouncing off, they could still find their way back.

What had happened was so clear to her now. She'd stood up at the regent's banquet in front of faculty and peers to accept the award she and Dash had won for their article exposing the hazing on Greek Row. Her speech had explained the *facts*— she'd sleuthed the story out and Dash had helped her. But the meaning Dash attached to her words was that she was giving him less credit than he thought he was due. Men hated that—it was the worst insult to their masculinity.

"Listen, I'm not goin' anywhere," Jim yelled, breaking into her thoughts. "I can stay here all night if I have to." His voice was rough, and Lauren could hear him gulping in between sentences. He was probably sitting in front of her door drinking a beer. Then he belched loudly and she knew she was right.

She was right about Dash, too. He had his pride and she'd crushed it. Not that she didn't deserve all the credit she'd claimed, but he deserved more than just her appreciation. He needed to be thought of as a great investigative reporter by his editor and the rest of the staff, and she'd taken that from him.

"On Tuesday, you're going to owe me two hundred and twenty-five more, got it?" came the slurred voice through the door. "No deals."

Lauren glanced at the purple windup alarm clock Winnie had given her when she'd moved out of the dorm. It was nearly eight P.M., and she'd promised to meet Faith back on campus so they could go to a free showing of *The Rocky Horror Picture Show* at the student center.

But how was she going to escape? She was trapped in this depressing hole with her beer-guzzling landlord standing guard like a rabid Doberman.

"Four hundred and fifty dollars due Tuesday," the voice repeated.

Lauren felt a sudden chill, even though it was a warm night and the room was stuffy. Where in the world could she get that kind of money by Tuesday?

She read the next line in Dash's article, hoping it would give her some magical solution to her problem:

> *We all try really hard to listen, but sometimes, all we're hearing is the sound of our own voice.*

She pondered that a minute. Was she complaining too much, just listening to the bad parts of her life? She sat up suddenly, lifting her chin. She decided to block out the noise outside her door with positive thoughts. She would start working on the *Hers* column right now.

But as she picked up her yellow pad and started making a few notes for her own counterarticle, she felt overwhelmed. The walls of her cramped little room seemed to grow closer and more stifling around her. *Uh-uh, Lauren, let's hear some positives!* she thought to herself. Okay, at least she had a room.

But what was she going to do if she was thrown out on Tuesday?

Payday at the Springfield Mountain Inn wasn't till next Friday. By that time her last penny would surely have run out.

The landlord was ranting on about dumb kids who think they rule the world and just take, take, take. She put down her pad and clapped her hands over her ears. Things *had* to get better soon— didn't they?

"C'mon boy, come to Mama!" Liza whistled at Max, whose ears seemed to turn one hundred and eighty degrees in the direction of the shrill sound.

Then he lay down on the floor of the dorm room and his tail started beating the carpet like a jackhammer pounding out of control. Dust rose in the air.

"I've got to go, Liza. I'm meeting Lauren. The movie's about to start," Faith said. She put her working script of *Macbeth* on top of the pile of other scripts on her desk and started for the door. She really wanted to see Lauren and talk about all the rotten things that had happened lately so she could get some perspective on them.

"Now, just a sec." Liza jumped up and barred her way. Max jumped up with her. "I have to show you one more cute thing I taught him."

Why was Liza so dense? Faith had stated bluntly about four times in the past fifteen minutes that she was late and absolutely had to leave if she was going to meet Lauren in time for the movie.

Liza ignored her roommate's protests and made some kind of mumbo-jumbo hand signals at Max. Her false nails, painted a brilliant orange red to match her hair, caught Max's attention. He crouched, then leaped into the air, making a perfect four-point landing on Faith's bed, right on top of her neatly piled play scripts.

"Liza!" Faith screamed. "Now look what he's—"

"Good dog!" Liza praised, blowing a kiss at him and reaching into the canister on the shelf above her desk for a dog yummy.

"Get off, you beast! Scat!" Faith charged at Max, startling the poor animal so badly that he jumped off with a whimper.

Liza threw herself over him protectively. She glared at Faith. "Don't you dare hurt him! You're the beast," she yelled. She clucked at Max and stroked his tan fur. "Oh, darling, she didn't mean it."

Faith was livid. "Of course I did!" She stomped over to Liza's side of the room and kicked her brightly decorated theater trunk with one bare foot. "Ow!"

She sat down hard on the trunk and massaged her toe. "Look, we have to get rid of this menace, do you understand, Liza? We can't keep a dog here. It's against dorm regulations."

"But I love Max," Liza said. "I'll keep him out of your way. He stays in the room all day when we're at class or rehearsal."

"Exactly. And it's cruel to lock him up, Liza. He needs a home where he can run and play and roll in the grass and not chew everything in sight." She picked up a western civ textbook that had a neat row of tooth marks right down the spine and waved it in Lauren's face.

"He's so sweet!" Liza began.

"And he barks, too. He keeps people up at night and he's a dead giveaway. The first time Erin happens to be around when he lets loose one of those yowls, we're done for."

Liza narrowed her eyes. "It's not Max. You just hate me, that's all." She got up abruptly and swiped a stick of chewing gum off Faith's desk. She jammed the gum in her mouth and began chewing fiercely.

"Come on!" Faith's self-control was just about gone. She'd really had it with Liza's petty, selfish reactions. "You know everything I'm saying is right," she said. "Why do you have to act like such a brat?"

Liza's green eyes opened in innocent shock. "What a thing to call me! Now I see how you really feel. You just want me out of your room, out of your life. Well, I'm here to stay." Huge crocodile tears sprang to her eyes and began rolling down her cheeks.

"I want the dog out, not you," Faith said. She got up and walked to her desk, thinking that it would feel really great to scream. But the new, easygoing Faith wasn't supposed to do that. She retrieved the scripts that Max had knocked to the floor and tucked the rest of her pack of gum in the desk drawer.

"That's such a lot of hooey." Liza sniffed. "You hate me. You never thought I'd actually land a part in a classical play. You're just negative all the time, accusing me of getting you in trouble."

"But you did!" Faith said. "*You* burned candles in the room for atmosphere, *you* turned your boom box up to full volume—and *I* got blamed."

Liza didn't seem to hear a word Faith was saying. "I mean, I have done everything under the sun to make our friendship work," Liza raved on. "But obviously you're not interested. You know, the real reason I'm keeping Max is that at least he appreciates me. He doesn't turn his back on friendship like you do." Liza grabbed the huge black cape of her witch character off her closet hook and draped it dramatically around her ample body.

She headed for the door, but before she could throw it open, they both heard a single knock. The doorknob began to turn.

"Well, who's that?" Liza yanked the door open.

"Lauren!" Faith said, when she saw her old roommate. "I'm so happy to see you."

Liza glared at the newcomer. "Evidently you're more welcome here that I am," she huffed. "So I'm leaving. Come on Max."

Faith wanted to slam the door on her selfish

roommate, but instead she went over and closed it deliberately, then turned and leaned against it.

Lauren gave her a curious look. "What went on here?"

"Oh, don't ask. Liza and I are like oil and water. Or oil and fire. I don't know." Faith grimaced. She gathered her friend close for a hug.

Lauren hugged her back. "I decided to see if you were still here before going to the student center. I was cornered by my landlord about the rent and had to wait until he fell asleep to sneak out. How much of the movie have we missed?"

Faith glanced at her watch. "Not a whole lot. Let me get my boots on and we'll go."

She noticed that her closet door was open again. Liza had probably been looking for something to borrow. She felt around on the floor for her cowboy boots and dragged them out into the light.

"Oh, no!" she said, staring at them in open-mouthed horror. "I can't believe this!"

Lauren rushed to her side. "What happened?"

Faith held out the boots. Their buff pointed toes had been chewed so badly, the leather hung in frayed clumps. There was a ragged hole near the top of the right boot and tooth marks along the left boot's heel.

"Jaws!" Faith screamed. "That's what happened.

If Liza ever tries to bring that dog in here again," she bellowed, throwing the remains of her boots against the wall on Liza's side of the room, "I'm going to take a bite out of him! And enjoy doing it! "

Eight

"Okay, are you taking this jacket?" Peter Dvorsky asked, holding up a double-breasted black blazer.

"Maybe," KC responded vaguely. She pushed aside the curtains on her window and stared out at the trees that ringed Langston House, the girls-only dorm where she had a single. She had a blank stare on her beautiful face that Peter couldn't read. On KC's bed were various piles of clothing, books, and toilet articles. One pile was labeled *Go,* one labeled *Mail Home,* and one labeled *Who Knows?*

It was early Friday morning, the day before

Spring Formal. They were trying to clean out KC's tiny room and get all the final details finished before their plane left on Sunday. But every time Peter suggested chucking an item or shipping it back to Jacksonville, KC would tell him she couldn't make up her mind just yet.

Peter couldn't believe what a mess this room was. KC's wooden desk with its broken leg was leaning to one side from the weight of the boxes and books on it. Every inch of space on the floor was covered with something. And the bed was so littered with stuff that you couldn't even see the white-on-white quilt her grandma Rose had made her anymore. KC hadn't come to school with much—she didn't have a lot of things because she couldn't afford them—but the clutter managed to pile up anyway.

"Hey," Peter grumbled good-naturedly. "I'm tired. I already did my own packing. Why should I have to do yours?" He came up behind KC and tucked his hands comfortably into her skirt pockets.

She shrugged. "Okay. I'll get busy on it right away." But she didn't move from the window. "Have you packed all your cameras and tripods and stuff?" she asked, not sounding as though she really cared.

Peter moved his hands to encircle her delicate

waist. "I'll carry most of the photography stuff on board. KC?"

"Yes?"

"What's going on?"

"Huh?"

He took her by the shoulders and looked directly into her gray eyes. "We are about to start off on a great adventure together. I think we should level with one another."

She looked confused. "About what?"

"I know you pretty well—well enough to see that you're really rattled about something. So talk to me." He drew her close and kissed her lips softly once, twice, three times.

He could feel her pull away and he stood there, holding her hand, looking at her worried face. "Well?"

KC sank down on the bed, sitting on a pile of rolled-up socks. "Look, I've got to tell you something. It's so strange I can't really believe it happened. But it did."

Peter sat down next to her and put an arm across her shoulders. He had never loved anyone as much as he loved KC, and he couldn't bear to see her unhappy. "Tell me," he said.

"I saw Grandma Rose at the hospital yesterday," KC began.

Peter squinted at her. "*Your* grandma Rose?"

"Yes. Courtney and I were on our way to the Tri Beta house and we were passing the hospital. This woman in a hat looked so much like Rose that we followed her inside."

"So what happened?" Peter asked, stroking her back.

KC sighed. "We hung out on the side of the front hall and saw Rose go up to the receptionist. They talked and then went into a nearby room. As soon as they were gone I snuck over to the appointment book, and sure enough, there was Rose's name and a local phone number."

"What was she doing there?"

KC pressed her lips together. She shut her eyes tight and leaned back against Peter. "That's what I don't know. Why do people go to hospitals, Peter?"

"For their health, I'd say."

"Then you agree with me. You think she's sick?" KC asked, her voice shaking.

"Look, this is the best hospital in the area, right?" Peter said. "If I wanted to get a really thorough checkup—which I just might do if I were your grandma's age—this is where I'd go. She's probably getting one of those treadmill tests, having her knees and ankles knocked on, and having a little blood drawn. Then she'll be all done and she'll go home."

KC nodded, but she didn't look convinced.

"I can see you don't like my theory. Give me yours."

"Oh, who knows?" KC buried her face in his shoulder to hide the tears coming to her eyes.

Peter held her. He could feel how tense she was. "KC, I have this really direct approach to life. If I want to know something, I ask. You've got the phone number, so call. She'll answer the phone. You'll say, 'Hi, Grandma Rose, what are you doing in Springfield?' Then she'll tell you. Presto! Easy."

"You think so?" KC turned slowly to face him and he suddenly felt what she felt—uncertainty.

"I definitely know so," he said, trying to sound positive. "Give me the number. I'll dial it for you."

KC grabbed her purse off the windowsill and opened it, fumbling for her notebook. "Thanks, but I have to do it myself."

She stood up and headed for the door. "Will you come with me?"

Without speaking, they went into the hall. Two girls were leaning right up against the wall next to the hall phone, arguing about whether eating hot dogs every day for a year could kill you.

"How can eating hot dogs night after night not

be a guaranteed death sentence?" one girl wanted to know.

"You're wrong," the other girl said, "hot dogs are nutritious. If they were harmful, there'd be a warning label on them or something."

The first girl rolled her eyes. "That's so naive. I tell you—"

"Could you excuse us, please?" KC asked.

The girls didn't look up.

"I think hot dogs will only kill you if you put mayo and jelly on them," Peter said.

Both girls looked at him in horror.

"Just joking, but we would like to make an important phone call, so if you could please give us some privacy, we'd appreciate it." Peter smiled as the girls walked away. Then he reached in his pocket for a quarter. "Call's on me," he said to KC.

She took the coin, flipped it, and slapped it down on the back of her hand. "Heads, it's good news; tails, it's not," she said, trying to sound cheery.

Peter gave her a hug. She slid her hand off the coin and then she sighed.

"What'd you get?" Peter asked.

KC didn't answer. Instead she dialed the number written in her notebook and asked the hotel operator for a Rose Angeletti.

Peter watched her lift her hand to her mouth and bite a fingernail. She looked just like a little kid for a second.

"Hi! Grandma Rose, is that you?" KC asked, her voice slightly shaky. "It's KC. Yeah, really, it's me, I hope I didn't wake you up." She listened for a second and then said, "Oh, I have my ways of finding things out. You're pretty sneaky yourself, coming all the way to Springfield and not letting me know." She gave a forced little laugh.

"Well, of course I want to see you. Soon as possible. You know Peter and I are leaving for Italy next week. It'll probably be my last chance to get together with you."

She was listening again. Peter felt he was eavesdropping, but not really, since he could only hear one side of the conversation. Also, KC looked as if she really needed him.

He kept trying to figure out why Rose wouldn't have told her about being in town. Maybe she was just arranging a surprise family going-away party for KC. But that didn't explain Rose's visit to the hospital. What was going on?

"When can we do it?" KC was asking. "Oh, no. Tomorrow night's no good." She shook her head vehemently. "It's Spring Formal. That's kind of the social event of the year. Peter and I couldn't miss it. But how about the afternoon—would that be okay?" She listened, then nodded. "Fine. Tea it is. At your hotel at four P.M. No, let's make it three-thirty, so we have plenty of time to talk."

Peter grabbed her hand and she squeezed his. She looked a whole lot better now that she'd actually made contact.

"Oh, that's a great idea! Sure, I'd love for you to meet him," KC was saying. She grinned at Peter. "I know you'll be just as crazy about him as I am."

And then Grandma Rose said something else, and KC's face changed entirely. The wide dark eyes were suddenly shadowed, and her peachy complexion drained to a sickly white. "Okay," she said in a shaky voice. "See you tomorrow. Bye."

She hung up and replaced the receiver, but she wouldn't let go of it. Then she let out a strange, sad noise and started hurrying down the corridor, back to her room.

Peter sprinted to catch up with her. "Hey, wait a sec!" he called out. "What did Rose say? KC, talk to me." He got to the door just as she threw herself on the bed and buried her face in the pillow.

Peter sat beside her and took her in his arms, drawing her up in a close embrace. "KC, it can't be as bad as all that. What did she say?"

The tears had already come, and KC blinked a

few away as she looked at him. "Rose said . . . she said she wanted to be sure to meet you, since this might be her only chance." A huge sob racked her body and he held her while she wept.

"KC, calm down. I'm sure she just meant it was her only chance before we got on the plane." He stroked her hair and her back, trying without any luck to get her to stop crying.

KC shook her head and moaned a little. "From the minute I saw her walk into the hospital, I don't know why, but I've been certain there's something terribly wrong. Oh, Peter, what if she's dying? I couldn't bear it. I really couldn't."

Peter felt so helpless as she clung to him for support. There was nothing to say. All he could do was hope that she was wrong.

Winnie threw open the door of Josh's room at eight forty-five A.M. that morning. It was empty. The bed was unmade and there were clothes strewn everywhere. But the gremlin computer had its cover on. It appeared to be sleeping, and Winnie would be the last person to wake it up.

"So where is he?" she muttered, pulling off the sequined beret she was wearing and running a hand through the ends of her spiky hair.

They hadn't had a chance to talk since that awful phone call she'd made from the lab. Oh, she'd tried, but either he'd been at the library or too distracted to talk because of his killer computer project. And she was determined *not* to play second fiddle to a machine again. She knew Josh really wanted to hear her—his listening apparatus was just temporarily out of commission. But she had to fix that. She had to get through to him. Their "coupleness"—if there were such a word—was at stake.

If they didn't connect soon, Winnie was sure she'd do something drastic, something she'd regret for the rest of her life. All she wanted was for Josh to tell her that he *wanted* to see her tonight. Then she'd be saved. She wouldn't meet Dimitri and she'd have a chance to get things back together with Josh. Her mind would get screwed on straight again, and her emotions—well, they'd never be normal—but at least they would be back on their own crazy track. It was up to Josh now.

"Food," she decided. "He needs food at this hour."

She threw her bag with the Barbie dolls dangling from it over her left shoulder and made straight for the dining commons on the other side of

Forest Hall. It was a dank morning, overcast and chilly. She could feel the stiff breeze lift the tails of her white, oversized man's shirt, which she wore over orange-and-pink Day-Glo leggings. She shuddered a little and broke into a run so she could get there quicker.

The smell of bacon and doughnuts, mixed with the burned odor of coffee left too long on the hot plate, warmed Winnie up instantly. With all the bizarre feelings she'd been having lately, she didn't need coffee, though she dearly would have loved a cup. *I can get the caffeine shakes just by smell,* she told herself, looking around the crowded hall for a sign of Josh.

He was sitting by himself in the corner farthest away from the big picture window. She smiled at the sight of his unkempt long brown hair. He had on bleached-out jeans and a red T-shirt with a hole in the right shoulder. There was a dreamy look on his face—a look that always made her stop and be glad that he was a person who took the time to dream.

Winnie grabbed a box of cold cereal and a bowl and a spoon off the counter and got a carton of milk from the cooler beside it. With one forlorn glance at the coffee, she showed her meal card at the checkout line and then marched straight to Josh's table. She slid into the chair beside him.

"Saving this for someone? Or may I join you?" she asked.

Josh gave her a sleepy smile. "Join me, please."

"How are you, Josh?" she demanded. She tore open the little box and poured the contents into the bowl. "How are you, *really*?"

"Fine." He took a bite of the doughnut he was eating, and little specks of sugar dotted his mouth. She longed to kiss them off, but decided the moment wasn't right for smooching. She needed information.

"Look, I wanted to say that I'm sorry about that phone call the other day. I was in an awful mood and—"

"Win, you're always in some mood or other," he teased her lightly. "Sometimes they're awful and sometimes they're monstrous, and sometimes they're just downright strange."

This was good. She thought he sounded more open than he had lately. At least he was thinking about her moods.

"Well, I shouldn't have said all those things, I guess," she continued. "But neither should you. And I meant it about wanting us to do something together tonight. It's been so long since we had a little excitement."

As soon as she said the last word a picture of Dimitri, grinning at her over the mouse, came into her mind. Now there was an excitement expert if she'd ever met one.

"Well, I've got plans for tonight," Josh announced.

"Great, what are we doing?"

"Not we. Me. Sorry, Win, I'd promised Mikoto last week—"

Winnie was sure she'd heard wrong. "You're joking, right?"

"No, I really did make plans. Mikoto and I are going to hit the Zero Bagel first and hook up with some guys in my computer class. One of them is going to show us this new system he's designed that lets you call up about a thousand files with just one word."

Winnie's heart froze. As many times as Josh had been there for her, right now he was away. So far away she didn't quite know how he'd ever get back. Computer data obviously meant much more to him than dates with her.

"It must be fascinating," she said, doing a slow burn.

Josh sighed. Even in his present state of mind, he couldn't miss her tone of voice. "Look, Winnie, I'm not brushing you off. I just need this stuff for my project. And once that's done, I'm free."

"Good. Glad to hear it. When will that be?"

He shook his head. "I wish I knew."

Winnie swirled her spoon in the bowl of cereal. Her cornflakes spun around in the milk like ship-wrecked sailors looking for a life raft. She was looking for a raft, too. Her mind was made up.

She would meet Dimitri tonight at the Blue Whale. What else did she have to lose?

Nine

Melissa walked slowly up the marble steps of Honors College, not knowing what she was going to say to her adviser, Dr. Katzman. This was Melissa's semester review and she was dressed for the occasion in a pair of neatly pressed khakis and a starched black-watch-plaid shirt. Usually she tried to anticipate questions in order to have answers ready. But not this time. Her mind wasn't on her studies these days; it was on Brooks. *Brooks! What am I going to do about Brooks?* she asked herself.

A group of foreign students came racing out the front door of the building, waving some kind of banner written in a fancy Arabic script. Melissa dodged in time to avoid being knocked over. *I love Brooks,* she thought, *but I can't talk to him. He brings up the wedding and I feel like I'm itching all over, like I've got poison ivy or something.*

She glanced at her watch as she rushed down the hall to her adviser's ground-floor office. Only five minutes late.

Melissa knocked once and walked inside. The office had cinder-block walls and standard-issue desks and file cabinets, but the plants, Tiffany lamp, and two big posters of Degas dancers gave it a homey feel.

"Come in and sit down, Melissa," Dr. Eleanor Katzman, a petite woman wearing high black patent-leather heels and a pair of half glasses balanced precariously on the end of her nose, said as she looked up from her file folder. "I just read your report. Now tell me more about this public-health awareness day you want to sponsor in Springfield."

Melissa crossed her legs, then uncrossed them. Had she written such a report? Maybe Brooks would remember—she certainly couldn't.

"What areas are you really interested in? You've got everything from illegal garbage dumping to sexually transmitted disease here, and that's too much to cover."

Melissa twirled her coppery ponytail around one finger, looking at the dancers on the wall for an answer. "I guess the idea needs revamping."

Dr. Katzman pushed her glasses up on her nose. "I didn't say that. I just want particulars. Melissa?"

Melissa's mind was wandering. She noticed that the blinds were hanging unevenly, and she had this burning desire to get up and adjust the pull cord.

"Melissa, is something troubling you?"

"No, why?" Melissa answered immediately.

"You're not giving me answers. It's so unlike you."

"Sorry. I just wish . . ."

"Go on. What do you wish?" Dr. Katzman gave her a motherly smile—the kind Melissa wished her mother would give her once in a while.

"I wish I could figure out what comes first."

Dr. Katzman smiled. "Aha. The premed blues, right?"

Melissa finally got up and went to the window. Gingerly, she picked up the pull cord. "Until about three weeks ago," she began, "I was on top of all my courses. But then my coach for the track team said my times were getting slower, so I started training more hours. I'm exhausted. I fell asleep twice this week with my tracksuit on," she confessed.

"I can understand that," Dr. Katzman said. "Anything else?"

This was the hard part. Melissa had a lot of trouble talking about Brooks. "I'm getting married," she finally said, going back to her seat.

Dr. Katzman jerked up abruptly in her chair. "Are you? Soon?"

Melissa shut her eyes for a second, trying to think of the answer. But no good answer came. "I don't know. We haven't talked about it much."

"I see." Dr. Katzman stuck one hand in her lab-coat pocket and produced a roll of Life Savers. She popped one in her mouth and offered the roll to Melissa, who shook her head. "How about your families? Do they approve?"

"His, yes, I guess." Melissa's hands were damp, and she wiped them on her pants legs. "My family, well, I don't really know how my parents feel about my getting married."

"Did you ask them?" Dr. Katzman wanted to know.

"I'm going to. Really, I am," Melissa said. "See, my dad's just coming off some pretty hard times himself, and my mother just tells me how much work a good marriage takes. It sounds so hard."

Dr. Katzman went over to a photograph sitting on top of her file cabinet and took it down. She handed it to Melissa. "Your mother's right," she said. "It is a lot of work. Look at these people."

The picture was of a very young couple who were trying too hard to smile. They were holding each other around the waist and staring at the camera. In front of them was a double baby carriage, with two gurgling babies sitting side by side.

"It's you, isn't it?" Melissa said after a moment.

"Yes, it was taken right after the twins were born," Dr. Katzman explained. "I was in med school then."

Melissa looked up, surprised. "I never knew you went to med school."

"I dropped out after a year. My husband was there, too. A brilliant young neurosurgeon."

"You dropped out?" Melissa was horrified.

Dr. Katzman nodded. "Somebody had to take care of the babies, and the logical one was me. Who was I to say my career was more important than his?"

"But you *have* a career." Melissa pointed at the diplomas on the wall, and the award Dr. Katzman had won for an original DNA experiment she did in graduate school.

"But not the one I wanted," Dr. Katzman said softly. "When the twins went off to school, I decided I couldn't afford the time or the money to go back to medical school. So I went and got my Ph.D. in molecular biology and here I am!"

"But didn't your husband ever think that you—"

"My ex."

Melissa tried not to register shock, but it was hard. She loosened her grip on the photograph and it fell.

Dr. Katzman shrugged. "Yes, we got divorced. Don't get me wrong. I'm crazy about my kids. But at the time I resented them terribly. And I resented my husband for allowing me to make the sacrifice of giving up my dream for his."

Melissa wanted to cry. All the huge fears she'd been having lately suddenly blossomed, like ragweed in August.

Dr. Katzman sat on the arm of her chair. "I have to tell you this. Marriage is hard on everyone, but it's twice as hard at your age when you're just starting out in life and you have big goals—the both of you."

"You don't think I should marry Brooks?"

"I didn't say that." Dr. Katzman put a hand on Melissa's arm. "But it sounds like you and your young man have reached some kind of impasse. If you're really set on tying the knot, you have to be able to communicate with your partner. Med school is rough on the best marriages. Can you afford to risk losing one—or both?"

Melissa looked hopeless. She handed back the picture. "I don't want to mess up. I know I can't be perfect, but some part of me says I have to do well in school and run like crazy for my coach and make Brooks happy and my parents happy and—"

"What about yourself? Listen, your life isn't going to sort itself out in a day."

"I know that, but—"

"It's like your running," Dr. Katzman interrupted. "You couldn't go out there and do a marathon your first week in training. You had to build up endurance and stamina. So think of it as though you're in training to be a woman, Melissa. A little bit at a time. Not all at once. Got it?"

Melissa nodded slowly.

"Now get lost," Dr. Katzman said, smiling slyly. "Anytime you want to talk about your project—or anything else—let me know."

Melissa stood up and went to the door. "Thank you," she said stiffly.

As Melissa walked down the hallway she wondered briefly what Brooks would think about the conversation she'd just had with her adviser. She'd tell him all about it, really soon. And that would open the door to the rest of what they needed to talk about. And then everything would be all right. She hoped.

Ten

....

Faith rubbed her arms under the buckskin sleeves to keep warm. She would probably have turned into an icicle by now if it hadn't been for her sturdy, faithful old Daniel Boone jacket. The temperature in the "trap room" under the stage was about twenty degrees below the rest of the theater. It was like a root cellar down here.

If she lit the witches' caldron right now, she could probably warm up. *"Double, double, toil and trouble,"* she thought. Boy, would *she* ever be in trouble if she jumped the gun on this pot before Meredith or Briscoe asked for it. To make conditions more uncomfortable, the chemicals the prop guy had mixed with the dry ice smelled to high heaven. The whole thing looked like a disgusting oily concoction.

She heard footsteps overhead and the weight of one of the largest actors made the beams sag a bit.

"'Overweight Can Kill: Girl Is Crushed to Death in Stage Trap by Twinkie-eating Actor,'" she growled to herself.

"Okay, can you hear me, Faith?" Meredith's voice boomed in her ears.

"Loud and clear," she yelled back.

"Give it a try, would you?" he asked. "I want to make sure the trap is functional before we put the three witches on it for their supernatural entrance. Everyone," he called out, "clear the area around the trap, please. This is a check. Go ahead, Faith."

Faith reached up and released the hook that kept the trap secured to the floor when it wasn't in motion. Then she put her right hand on the trap lever, and with her left, she pushed the button that started up the mechanism. She heard a deep rumbling as the wooden piece, reinforced with steel, began to move.

"All the way up now," Meredith told her.

She yanked on the lever with steady pressure, bringing the trap level with her head, then up some more so that it cleared the ledge and came even with the floor of the stage. It occurred to her that except for her fingers, which were still entirely numb, she was actually warm from the effort.

Faith heard Briscoe's pearly tones from the middle of the theater. "Meredith, would you ask her to raise it higher? Might be nice to lift the witches above the stage and have them jump off. The smoke from the caldron should probably cover their feet. They'll look like they're flying. Give it a go, would you?"

"Did you hear that, Faith?" Meredith asked.

"Yes. I don't know how far up this thing goes," she said, pulling harder on the lever. "I hope I don't throw it out of whack." It gave a little. Then she threw all her weight into it and yanked with both hands. The platform jerked up another four feet.

"Good. Excellent! All right, take it down, light the caldron and get those witches on board," Briscoe ordered.

Faith could feel the calluses growing on the insides of her palms as she manipulated the lever. Electrical or not, it took a lot of strength to work the trap. As it came back to ground zero beside her, she took a breath, then got her packages of dry ice ready.

She heard voices. Liza, and the other two witches, Susan Abernathy and Nicky Carlucci, were coming in from the property room next door to the trap.

"Ooh, is this spooky!" Nicky said as she walked inside. Nicky was wearing a rehearsal costume that looked like a lot of strips of black fabric torn in tatters. Her face was smudged with carbon from a burned cork to give her a grimy, mean look.

Nicky was followd by Susan. "Ow, I hit my head. It's so low in here," Susan complained. Faith had heard Merideth say that Susan would never have gotten the part of Witch Two if she hadn't been nearly six feet tall. The costume designer had accentuated Susan's height by having her wear wooden clogs under a swirling black cape, and a huge crushed velvet hat that looked like a smashed pizza on her head.

As soon as Liza came in she started coughing. "Yuk, what is that smell?" she asked.

"It's the chemicals on the dry ice," Faith explained.

"Well, I can't say my lines if I can't breathe, and I can't breathe with that junk in my lungs." Liza gagged dramatically, waving the broom she carried as a prop to clear the air. Then she yanked the black hood of her cloak off her mass of red ringlets, and Faith noticed that they looked slightly damp, as though Liza had been sweating all through rehearsal. "Faith, *do* something about the smell, would you?"

Faith did get a kick out of seeing Liza so upset. Now maybe her roommate would have an inkling of what it felt like when Max chewed up her boots. Liza could make the biggest fuss of anyone she knew about anything—big or small.

"What would you like me to do?" Faith asked. "The caldron's in the script. It's got to smoke; it's got to stink, or else Mr. Briscoe will be very disappointed. Not to mention how upset William Shakespeare would be."

"All right!" she heard Meredith's voice again. "What's going on down there?" There was a tapping on the ceiling right above them. "We haven't got all day, girls."

"It's dark here, Meredith," Susan yelled up. "We can't exactly figure out where—"

"Faith, help them out. We have a lot to cover today and I want to keep this rehearsal moving."

Faith gave her hand to each of the witches in turn and helped them onto the trap platform. "Ready?" she asked. "I'm going to start up the caldron." She looked at the caped figures huddled together and was reminded of three big crows perched on a branch.

"Okay, let's have it," Liza said brusquely. "I'll breathe through my mouth."

"Good idea, there's lots of hot air in there already," Faith said under her breath.

She opened the two dry-ice packets and threw them simultaneously onto the oily surface of the big pot. It immediately took on a life of its own, the waves of thick smoke issuing from all sides. Then she started to raise the trap.

"Oh, no, I can't stand this!" Liza screamed. She grabbed Nicky's arm and shut her eyes tight, gasping for air like a fish out of water. "It's going too fast! Slow it down!"

"Ssh!" Faith yanked on the sleeve of her robe. "Nicky, you keep her still while I send you upstairs. Hold on."

She started pulling on the lever. Susan and Nicky gave little gasps, but Liza, of course, let out with a yell that could have been heard in the second balcony.

"Liza, shut up!" Faith shouted. "You're hardly traveling ten feet. That's less than one story of a building."

"A building! Oh, NOOO!" Liza's voice came out in a long, shaking soprano note. "I'm going to faint."

"Come on, now," Faith encouraged her, "it's

not that bad. Once you get used to this, you'll love it. It's like going on a ferris wheel for the first time."

"I loathe and despise amusement-park rides." Liza dug the nails of her hand into Susan's shoulder, and the poor girl yelped.

Liza was panicking. "I'm terrified of heights," she screamed.

"Liza, cut it out. Let's get going," Faith said. She pulled the lever back farther.

Smoke filled the tiny trap area, and Faith could feel her eyes stinging. The three witches were all coughing now, and who could blame them? Faith felt sick, too. She'd pass out if she had to smell this stuff every night of the run.

The rumbling platform moved slowly, with a stop-and-go motion. Faith couldn't help thinking that the mechanism was as faulty as her roommate.

"Higher, Faith!" she heard Briscoe call.

Faith gave the lever her best shot and sent the thing lurching upward. It was about one foot past stage level when it jammed and then suddenly dropped about two feet, coming to a halt with a sickening thud.

"Oh, God, I'm going to die!" Liza shrieked, clutching the side of the smoking caldron.

"Liza, let go of the pot!" Faith called to her.

"Somebody, help me!" Liza wailed as she held on for dear life. "This is all your fault, Faith. You did it on purpose because of Max! I hate you!" She crouched down to get her balance, holding on to the big pot. Then, as Faith watched, horrified, Liza lurched toward the edge of the platform, still keeping her white-knuckled grip on the caldron.

"Liza, let go of that, it's going to tip!" Faith screamed.

It was too late. Liza jumped, bringing the huge stinking pot tumbling into the trap with her.

Faith immediately felt the drenching mess cover her hair, her shoulders, her arms, her entire body. She was completely doused and stinking from head to toe.

"Mr. Briscoe." Liza was sobbing and coughing in a corner of the trap room. "Meredith—someone!—come and get me!"

Faith coughed and spit out the bitter taste of the liquid in her mouth. Her whole body was shaking. If she could have ripped off her clothing, she would have. "You have the nerve to complain, Liza!" she said, blinking her eyes wildly. "Just look at me. Look at what you did to me!"

The oily, smoky, revolting mix was running

down the back of Faith's neck. She tried to hold her breath against the chemical smell, but it did no good. It was in her nostrils and her mouth. Billows of dry ice rose around her.

"What is going on!" Meredith's face appeared around the corner of the trap, along with those of Susan and Nicky, who had easily stepped off the platform onto the stage when it got stuck.

"I can't believe she did that to me," Liza started up again. Her face was streaked with tears and her mascara ran down her cheeks in two long black ribbons. She dabbed at her eyes with the hem of her cape. "I need a glass of water, something . . . I'm terrified. I'm having a breakdown. I'll never climb on anything higher than a footstool, I swear. My heart must be going about ninety miles an hour."

Faith was numb, unbelieving, as she stared at her ruined jacket. There was hardly an inch of it that wasn't stained with the oil slick.

She reached over and pressed the off button on the trap mechanism. Then she hoisted herself up onto the jammed platform, as much to get away from Liza's sobbing as anything else. She felt like sobbing herself, but she wouldn't. Couldn't. She'd been so professional, so calm. She'd worked away on this production despite Briscoe's petty meanness and Erin's jealousy and Liza's craziness. But this was too much.

"Quiet, everyone!" Briscoe's voice boomed around the theater. He was striding around the stage, looking through the smoke down into the trap. "Faith, did you turn the platform mechanism off, at least?"

Faith clenched her teeth. "Yes, sir."

"Well then, you go back in that trap with some rags and towels and clean up that mess. Meredith, we need the maintenance man. You should have checked this out before we were in rehearsals. Time is of the essence. Faith, what are you standing around for? Get busy!" Briscoe barked.

Faith's insides were churning. She climbed down inside the foul-smelling trap and went to find some rags, even though she was so incredibly angry—at Briscoe, at Liza, at that dumb dog Max, at Erin—that she could have lifted all of them and thrown them right inside the smoking caldron.

Everything in her life was utter chaos, a total mess, disgusting and smelly and awful. Her carefree, devil-may-care attitude was gone. The rage inside her had been simmering like the caldron full of gunk. If Scott didn't get back home the next night for Spring Formal, if something good didn't happen in the next twenty-four hours, she was set and ready to explode.

Eleven

"**Y**ou don't mind if I don't come with you, do you?" Josh asked Mikoto, his roommate. He rubbed his tired eyes as the streetlight outside the Zero Bagel blinked on. It seemed bright as day in his beat condition.

Mikoto shrugged. "No problem. I'll check out the computer system for you," he said as he unlocked his bicycle from the rack and climbed on. "You've been working too hard. Why don't you find Winnie now that your project's done. Go to a movie."

Josh smiled and nodded as he watched Mikoto ride off. Finding Winnie and being with her was indeed his first priority. They needed time together. Real time, not chatter time.

He leaned against the side of the building, thinking about her brown eyes, filled with love, flashing with fury, giggling with fun. She was something. He couldn't believe how lucky he was to have met her. Winnie kept his head on straight.

So where was Winnie right this very second? He pulled himself upright, then put one foot in front of another, making himself move. Like an idiot he'd told her that he was going to be busy tonight, so maybe she'd decided to put in some time at the Crisis Hotline. That would be a great place to look for her.

"Hello, Josh!" A couple waved at him as he started up the block.

He didn't even recognize them. "Hi!" he said, nodding and slogging on. He'd never felt so exhausted.

Why had he pushed himself so hard on this project? It was important, sure, and he wanted a good grade, but he was doing fine in Professor Ransom's class anyway. It was more like he had to prove to himself that in spite of computer glitches and no sleep, he could be the best. He could make it happen. He could make anything happen if he wanted it enough.

What he wanted now was to get Winnie back.

He felt so lonely without her. He couldn't remember when they'd last had the chance to sit under the night sky and count stars. It was like he'd pushed her outside his world. How could he have done that to the person he thought of as his second self?

He had just turned onto The Strand, which was one of the fanciest blocks in Springfield. The exclusive Blue Whale Restaurant was on the corner, and he happened to glance through the lace-curtained window.

A couple was holding hands and their heads were bent toward each other. They reminded him of the way things used to be between himself and Winnie.

He blinked and stopped. He *really* must be tired! That girl in the window looked so much like Winnie.

No, that was impossible. What would she be doing here? With a guy?

He pulled back a little to get a better look at the face slightly hidden by the curtain draped across the window. The girl's features were highlighted by a small porcelain lamp sitting on the table.

Oh, no. Josh felt as if his blood were being drained out of his body.

That was Winnie. His Winnie. She was wearing

this amazing clingy dress he'd never seen before, made out of some fabric that glowed blue green in the dim light.

For a second his legs gave and he had to support himself against the wall. Seeing Winnie with another guy made him physically ill.

She was leaning across the table at her dinner partner, so Josh tore his eyes away from her to do the same.

The guy was older, maybe twenty-five or twenty-six. Josh had never seen him before, but he had a look that Josh instantly disliked—a look that said, *I think I'm God's gift to women.* His dark hair was well cut and groomed, he wore an expensive sport jacket over a black T-shirt. He had a scar near his left eye and really big hands. Those hands were holding one of Winnie's.

Josh made a fist and jammed it into the opposite palm. "Damn!" he said. He couldn't believe this. This wasn't happening! Winnie, out with another guy?

Why hadn't she said something, for God sakes! Josh felt his breath coming in hard, angry spurts. He couldn't get enough air. He stared at the guy. He stared at Winnie.

She had an expression on her face that Josh knew all too well. He'd seen it on dreamy nights when the two of them took walks around the campus. But she was giving this guy the exact same look! And she just about melted when he flashed one of his sexy, lopsided smiles that put one dimple in his cheek.

"Winnie, so help me . . . What in the name of—" Josh felt stunned, outraged, beside himself with jealousy, and completely crushed.

He wanted to turn away, but his eyes were glued to Winnie, who was hanging on every word that fell out of the guy's mouth. She liked this person, thought he was interesting, exciting.

Josh hated him. But he hated himself even more for having turned Winnie away so many times, for having told her in so many words that she didn't count as much as his computer project.

He had to do something, but what? Feeling dizzy and feverish, he walked to the door of the Blue Whale and put his hand on the polished brass knob. Just as quickly, he pulled it away. Although he had to take the blame for driving Winnie into the arms of another guy, *she* was the one who had betrayed their love and trust. If he went inside, he knew he wasn't going to get down on his knees and beg her to forgive him. He was going to cause a bad scene. He was going to punch the guy. And he was going to scream at Winnie that it was over.

"The end." Josh said the words out loud in a

dull, stunned voice. Then he took one last look through the window at Winnie and walked off into the night.

"You're not hungry?" Dimitri asked, taking Winnie's hand and stroking her fingers.

She looked down at her plate. She'd cut up the chicken and pushed the wild rice around, but she was too nervous to eat. What was she doing? If Josh knew she had a date with someone else, let alone was about to do something wicked, he'd probably disavow knowing her.

She gave Dimitri what she hoped was a cool shrug. "I've had enough. This food's awfully rich."

"I agree." He held her with those fabulous eyes of his, questioning her without words.

"Yes," she answered. "I'm okay. I'm ready now." Her voice was slightly shaky because it was time to do the wicked deed—something she'd never done in her life. She was about to run out of a restaurant without paying the bill.

It was an incredible risk, but Winnie was up for it. After all, she'd already taken a big risk by getting together with another guy. The only difference was you could always pay back money if you

had to, but once you squandered the most important relationship of your life, there was seldom a
second chance.

Winnie tried to push all thoughts of Josh out of
her mind as Dimitri pulled her chair out and
helped her up. The bill was lying right on the
table, inside one of those great-smelling leather
folders that the woman was never supposed to see.

"I'm proud of you," Dimitri whispered. He took
her hand and ran his index finger around her palm,
sending shivers through her body. "You've got guts."

Three waiters were hovering over the next table,
one carving pork roast, the other ladling out three
different sauces in a curving pattern around the
side of some woman's plate. The last was serving a
gigantic niçoise salad.

Before Winnie could think too much about the
stunt they were about to pull, she walked swiftly
to the ladies' room and locked the door behind
her.

There was a fancy brass catch on the small window over the sink. If she could get the window
open, she could climb out, just like Dimitri had
told her to. She yanked at it, but it wouldn't give.
Was this a sign that she was making a horrible mistake? Suppose someone came in right now?
Winnie, think! This is not a joke. You could get into

some serious trouble here. What are you trying to prove?

She couldn't answer that one, so she decided to give the window one more try. If it didn't work, she'd go right back into the restaurant and—but then the catch suddenly budged. There! It was open!

Winnie hiked her dress up high enough so that she could climb out. Her pulse was racing as fast as it had that night in the cemetery. Blocking out any and all thoughts except her escape, she boosted herself up on the sink. The coast was clear out the window.

"Psst! I'm out of the men's room," Dimitri whispered from outside. "Are you coming?"

"Hold on," she whispered back.

Quickly, she took off her shoes and hurled them down to the ground. They made a dull, thudding noise, and she wondered how far that carried on the night air. But there wasn't time to worry. She stuck one leg out, then one arm, then wedged her small body through the opening. She landed on her feet as perfectly as a cat.

Then Dimitri grabbed her arm. "I've got your heels, but don't put them on," he said. "Run barefoot, we'll go faster."

She felt the wind against her face and she moved

faster than she ever had before. *We did it! We did it!* she thought as they raced through the night like shooting stars through the sky. Dimitri was right! She could do anything.

"That was fabulous!" Dimitri was practically shouting. "I love this! Winnie, we skipped out on the bill and no one knew! We are so incredibly clever."

Winnie wanted to be clever, but in the next second she had an awful thought. Every crime is perfect—until the criminal is caught. In just a few more seconds the waiter would come back to the table and find the leather wallet didn't have any money inside. He would tell the maître d' and they'd start a search. Josh would find out. He'd know she was with somebody else. He would loathe the very sight of her.

The thought ate right into her. Winnie felt her heart racing, but it wasn't with excitement anymore. They'd broken the law! They could be arrested! She could lose Josh! She was overcome with guilt and terror so intense, she felt her breath catch in big heaving sobs.

"Faster, Winnie. There's the campus. It's like we never left. This is so sweet, isn't it?"

Josh would see her in the papers, but not for any reason she'd be proud of. It would be a mug shot.

She'd have a police record. He'd never want to speak to her again. Oh, how could she have done this!"

"Dimitri, I can't—"

"Of course you can! You just did! Winnie, I am crazy about you!"

They were running along the perimeter of the campus, about three blocks from the medical school. A bank of beech trees, heavily laden with their spring foliage, bent over them as they passed by. Several branches caressed Winnie's face as she raced under them. At any other time she would have been calmed by the feeling, but tonight they felt like tentacles, reaching out to grab her.

Guilty as charged. She could see the look on Josh's face when he read the Springfield newspaper. She had to forget it. It was done now, there was nothing she could do to take back the last two hours.

They sped across McClaren Plaza, their feet pounding hard on the granite. The tiny chips of mica sparkled in the moonlight.

"Over here," Dimitri called. His long shadow was highlighted by the streetlights. He stood still, with his hands in the pockets of his tailored slacks. He wasn't even breathing hard, as though he'd just taken her out for a stroll in the moonlight.

She felt pulled toward his powerful body and moved closer.

Running both hands down her arms, he whispered, "Want to go up in the tower with me?"

Winnie shivered at his touch, and at the very thought of the tower. It was an old crumbling structure at the back of the plaza that had been in place since before the university was built. The tower was made of massive, multicolored rock pieces that sat at jagged angles all the way up to the top. Long ago, the police had nailed a few boards over the entrance, but daredevil students climbed up inside anyway, just for the thrill. Once you got to the top, you could look out over the whole campus.

"Have you ever climbed up here?" he asked.

"Uh-uh." She wanted to. She didn't want to.

"Come on, we'll go together."

Winnie looked at him—really looked. There was something so appealing about his wide-eyed excitement that she got caught up in the game again. "Okay, let's do it," she agreed. Maybe the heights would clear her mind.

He helped her climb through the opening between the boards and they started up the circular stone staircase. It was musty and damp inside.

The climb was steep. It must have taken five

minutes to get to the top. They leaned against the edge, panting a little for breath. Dimitri turned her gently to face him.

"You are so wonderful," he breathed softly. "There's nothing you won't do."

And suddenly his mouth was close to hers and she felt a wonderful rush of delirium. She closed her eyes to everything but the moment. It was electrifying. He drew back and began to pull her out on the ledge.

"Dimitri!"

"Let's walk around the whole ledge. We can do it! We can do anything!"

She bit her lip, trying not to think. If she stopped here, she'd kick herself forever for being a coward. It was crucial, somehow, that she do something with Dimitri she could never do with Josh. She had to try, after all, or risk being boring.

Carefully, she put one stockinged foot up on the highest stone and pulled herself up until she was standing. Then she made the mistake of looking down.

She sucked in air. "We're so high," she said. "What if we fall?"

"Just don't look at the ground, Winnie. Now, come on."

Winnie slid her left foot out, then dragged the right behind her. She was still terrified, but she watched Dimitri glide along the ledge and tried to copy him. As she picked her foot up again she felt a sickening lurch and she lost her balance.

"Dimitri, help!" she yelled as her hands groped for something—anything—to hold on to. There was nothing to save her. She was falling through space; she was going to topple off the tower and plunge to her death.

Suddenly she felt his strong hands pulling her back. She landed hard inside the ledge, on the floor of the tower. She felt bruised, as though she might start crying at any minute. Why had she done that? How stupid could a person be? No wonder Josh didn't want to spend time with her anymore. She was physically and morally and emotionally stupid!

Dimitri was leaning over her. He kissed her forehead, then stroked her hair. "You've got to trust me," he said. "I would never let anything bad happen to you, okay? But when you're in for thrills, you have to swing with the punches. This was nothing. You're fine; I'm fine."

"I thought . . . I thought I was going to die," Winnie murmured in a very small voice. Risking everything, she'd practically killed herself. Maybe it served her right. Her knee was all bloody, and she was shaking inside and out. Over and over again she felt that awful sensation of falling into a void, falling away from everything she loved, everything that mattered—most of all Josh.

"This is nothing," she heard Dimitri say. "Tomorrow's the real test. Tomorrow we attempt the big one."

She began to shake her head, but he wouldn't let her say no to him. It was the way he looked at her that made her do crazy things. Josh always gave her room, let her make up her own mind. But this guy—he was all over her, stuck on her skin and in her pores. She lost her will when she looked into his eyes.

"Want to hear about the ultimate adventure?" he went on.

Winnie felt like a kid again, without control, without limits. With Josh, it was easy to make decisions, figure out what she wanted. With Dimitri, her mind was always spinning one way and then the other. No decision was easy. But she didn't have to go over the edge—she hadn't a few minutes ago. "Okay, what?"

"I know this mountain chalet," Dimitri said. "We can sneak up there and spend the night. The whole night, till dawn."

Winnie got goose bumps. It wasn't like he'd show her to the guest room and give her a good-night kiss on the cheek. Would she be able to make up her mind right then between betraying Josh and plunging into something wild and incredibly exciting with Dimitri? "You mean you have a friend who'll lend you the key?"

Dimitri gave her one of his lopsided, sexy smiles. "I can 'borrow' the key. No problem. How does nine o'clock sound? I'll tell you where to meet me."

Before she could even think what she was going to answer, he was kissing her again. Long, slow kisses that made her feel all bubbly.

Tomorrow night she'd really wanted to go to Spring Formal with Josh. But what were her chances of that? Josh was either going to be pounding on his keyboard or talking about new programs with his buddies. She had to face it— Josh just was not there for her anymore. She couldn't count on him.

Anyway, a dull old formal was something that boring people went to. Dimitri was offering her the moon and stars. There simply wasn't a choice.

"Sure, that sounds fabulous. I'd love to."

And she meant it.

She wanted to be everything Dimitri said she was—daring, exciting, mysterious, wonderful.

And she would be.

Twelve

....

With every step that Faith took on the sunny dorm green, she heard girls talking about which nail-polish color they were going to try, whether to pin their hair up or keep it down, whether to wear heels or flats.

"Who cares!" Faith muttered, kicking a clod of green out of the beautifully manicured lawn.

Spring Formal was only hours away and she still had no word from Scott. This didn't surprise her since everything had gone wrong for weeks now, and Faith had no reason to believe it was going to change by the time the dance started.

"I do."

She heard a voice behind her and whirled around. It was Kimberly Dayton, wearing her usual leotard and tights with a big scarlet shirt tied in a knot at her hip. Her hair was in beaded cornrows, which accented her high forehead and striking dark eyes. Kimberly lived next door to Faith in Coleridge, and the two of them had become really good friends through their work in the theater department.

"Oh, hi, Kimberly. Don't mind me," Faith said. "I'm just having that kind of day. How've you been?"

"Pretty good. But I think I have bad news for you." Kimberly pulled Faith down beside her on the grass and gracefully folded her legs tailor style.

"Great. I guess I shouldn't expect anything else."

Kimberly rubbed Faith's arm in a gesture of sympathy. "I happened to be passing the dorm phone when it rang. Scott called."

"He did?" Faith had one second of hopefulness.

"His team won, so they've got another game tonight."

"Oh."

Kimberly had a pained expression on her face. "You were supposed to go to the dance with him, weren't you?"

Faith cleared her throat. "I didn't really want to go to Spring Formal. It's so . . . formal," she murmured bravely. "And me, well, I'm casual."

"Listen, why don't you come with me and Derek?" Kimberely suggested.

"Thanks," Faith said, shaking her head. "But I don't think I'd be much fun."

"I understand. And to change the subject, I brought a letter for Lauren that someone sent to her old room. Can you give it to her?"

"Sure." Faith tucked the envelope in the back pocket of her jeans and quickly got to her feet. "I've got to go."

She felt waves of disappointment wash over her as she blurted out a good-bye and started back toward Coleridge. *It's not fair!* she wanted to yell. *Why can't something nice happen to me for a change?* She'd tried—really tried—to take everything as it came, on the chin. But she was reeling from the punches now.

She was missing Spring Formal, her favorite clothes were ruined, she didn't have Lauren around to make her feel better. And worst of all—tomorrow afternoon, she was going to have to spend three more hours in that smelly trap room.

When she threw open the door to her room, she stared in disbelief. Liza was curled up on her bed with none other than Max. She was wielding a big-toothed grooming comb through Max's scraggly fur. Faith's bed was totally covered with dog hair.

Faith snapped. "Liza, if you like dog fur and fleas so much, why don't you comb him on your own bed?"

She walked briskly to the two of them and yanked on Max's collar. He slinked over to crawl under her bed and stayed there with his head between his paws.

"You really have no feelings," Liza yelled at Faith. "Max needed something nice after the awful day he's had."

Faith began trying to gather up the dog fur, but the soft hair rose into puffballs above her bed and settled again. "What terrible thing happened to him today?" she demanded.

"Well, he's been given notice. Or at least, we have," Liza said casually, unpinning the note that she'd tacked to Faith's bulletin board. She handed it to her.

Faith blinked as she recognized Erin's elaborate script on the piece of paper.

WARNING: Faith Crowley and Liza Ruff are hereby given first warning. Dorm rules

require that no animals be sheltered on the
premises. Any evidence that the dog found in
Room 219 has not been removed will be cause for
both girls being put on probation.

This was it. The very last straw. With a growl
that came from deep within her, she hurled the
paper at Liza.

"You get rid of that dog in one hour," she
yelled, "or I swear, Liza, I'll take him right to the
dog pound."

Liza started to say something, but Faith went to
the bulletin board over her desk and removed a
pushpin. She held it up like a weapon.

"Don't you hurt me!" Liza whimpered, dashing
for the door.

Faith stared at her. Liza was afraid of her, just as
she had been on the moving platform when Faith
was in charge. She suddenly got a rush of power.
It felt okay to be angry. Actually, it felt great.

"And the instant I hear one more snotty comment out of you during *Macbeth* rehearsals," Faith
went on, her voice getting stronger, "I will pur-
posely get you stuck on the trap lift and leave you
there!" She stabbed the pushpin back into the
board.

Liza's wide green eyes opened in shock. "All

right. Okay! I'll get rid of Max."

"Now!" Faith shouted.

Liza immediately got her cape and the leash and dragged Max, yowling and yelping, toward the door.

"You're going to regret this," Liza said, but she was too frightened to sound convincing. Staggering a little in her high-heeled white boots, she got out of there as fast as she could.

Faith closed the door behind them and leaned against it, her heart rate going triple time. Incredible! Her fury had really accomplished something. The dog—and Liza—were gone.

She let her body sink on its own until she was sitting cross-legged on the floor. *Oh, Scott, why couldn't you have lost the stupid game?* she thought. And only then did she let one tear roll down her cheek.

"Grandma Rose said she'd meet us in the lobby," KC told Peter. She felt unsteady on her feet, so she tucked her arm into Peter's as they walked up the steps of the Pennbrook Hotel. It was one of those old, elegant places with over-stuffed sofas and morris chairs in the lobby. There were lovely brass lamps on little mahogany tables and heavy brocaded draperies at each window.

"That's got to be her, right?" Peter pointed across the room. "Neat hat."

KC felt her palms become damp. "Grandma Rose!" she called.

Rose was wearing a soft gray hat angled down over one side of her face. As she got up to hug KC the spray of brownish-red feathers tucked into the band brushed KC's face.

"Oh, it's so good to see you!" KC said, hugging her grandmother tight. She breathed in Rose's spicy scent and prayed that she was all right. Surely a woman who felt this strong couldn't be sick? Or could she?

"My goodness, you look beautiful. How are you?" Grandma Rose said. Before KC could answer, Rose pulled away and drew Peter toward her with one gloved hand. "You wouldn't be Peter, would you?"

Peter grinned, tugging his tweed jacket down in back. He shook her hand. "Nice to meet you, Mrs. Angeletti."

"No, don't call me that! I'm just Rose to you." She rubbed her white-gloved hands together, and her bright gray eyes, so like her granddaughter's, sparkled with mischief. "Let's go inside and eat some rich cake with plenty of icing that your father would throw in the garbage."

"You think I can get mine to go?" Peter asked as they walked toward the dining room. They could hear a string quartet playing classical music. "I hate to do this, Rose, but I have a test, and I have to be back on campus soon. I'm playing catch-up so my adviser can transfer some credits for me when I get to Italy."

"Tests on Saturday! Unheard of!" Rose clucked as the captain seated them at a table near a window. "We'll be sorry to lose your company, but that gives me and KC all the more time to gossip about you."

"Fine with me," Peter said, smiling. He took KC's hand across the table.

Rose took off her gloves with a flourish and waved to the waiter, who zipped over instantly. "The ladies will have tea and chocolate cake, and please wrap up most of what you've got on the pastry tray for this growing young man here," Rose told him, tucking a lock of her soft white hair back under her hat.

She turned to Peter. "Now tell me quickly all about your wonderful scholarship," she said.

KC glanced from her grandmother to Peter and back again. They really liked each other! The sound of their voices as they chatted together almost drowned out the anxious thoughts KC was having about why Rose had been at the hospital.

Peter glanced at his watch. "Well, I feel awful about this," he said to Rose once the waiter returned with a pastry-filled box for him to take, "but my time's up." He pushed back his chair and stood up. "It's been a real pleasure," he said, giving Rose his hand.

She didn't shake it, but drew him close and kissed his cheek. "You take care of this precious granddaughter of mine," she threatened, "or you'll answer to me when you get home."

"It's a deal," he agreed. He came around the other side of the table to kiss KC's cheek. "I love you," he whispered. "Stop worrying." Then he vanished out the restaurant door.

KC suddenly felt shaky again. She had to know, immediately, or something inside her was going to burst.

"What a nice young man. I'm glad for you," Rose spoke first. She picked up her teacup and lifted it as if to sip from it, but then she put the cup down again.

Then Rose's face changed totally. KC could actually see her aging, as if she had taken off a mask and was allowing her real emotions to show. "Oh, KC," Rose said in a voice so quiet it was difficult to hear.

KC knew immediately that every fear she'd had was coming true.

She took her grandmother's hands in hers. "Please, Grandma, tell me. Are you ill?" she asked.

Her grandmother's steely-gray eyes peered at her. It was as though she were measuring KC's ability to take bad news. "Darling, listen to me, and believe me. I'm fine. Just fine."

KC was shaking her head. Her hands were ice cold. "No, it's not true. You come to Springfield without even telling me, and park yourself at this out-of-the-way hotel where you think no one will find you." Her voice was strained, but the words kept spilling out. "And then, I happen to see you walking into the hospital."

Rose jerked her head up. "You saw me?"

"Yes, I followed you inside. And I saw your name in the appointment book," KC went on. "So don't try to tell me you're fine, Grandma Rose. Just tell me the *truth*!"

Rose gripped KC's hands tighter. She looked away from her granddaughter's stricken face, but there was no hiding the dismay in her eyes. "I had hoped to keep it from you just a little longer, but that's not very fair of me, is it? We've always told each other everything."

KC's shoulders ached, and there was a humming

in her ears. She didn't want to hear. But she had to.

"Sweetheart," Rose said in a flat voice, "your father has lung cancer."

KC knew that something important had just been said. Something terribly crucial that would affect her entire life. But it simply wouldn't penetrate. She crossed her legs, then uncrossed them. She shut her eyes tight.

"Did you hear what I said?" Rose asked.

KC's head was filled with images: her father pushing her on a swing, her father holding her when she fell, her father baking her a triple-layer chocolate birthday cake.

"No," she said. "No, no, NO!" The words ripped from her in a painful moan. She couldn't weep, couldn't even breathe. She was numb.

"I brought him to Springfield about two weeks ago for tests," Rose said softly, putting one soft, veined hand on KC's cheek. "When we got the results, I thought I should speak with the specialists in person."

"Not Daddy . . . not him." KC was pleading to make the awful word her grandmother had said go away.

"Your father didn't want you to know anything about this until he was ready to tell you himself.

And he didn't feel up to making the trip a second time."

KC stood up quickly, knocking over her teacup. Her grandmother was right behind her, and she caught KC before she could fall. With an arm around her shoulders, she eased her back down in the chair again.

"It's a mistake," KC said frantically. "Those were somebody else's tests. Not Daddy's."

"I know what you think." Rose sighed heavily. "Your father never put anything into his body that would harm him. No cigarettes, no pollutants. Well, the type of cancer he has is caused by scars on the lungs."

"How would he get . . . ?" KC's head was pounding. She put her hands up to her temples as if to press all the awful thoughts out.

"Remember when he got so sick about five winters ago?"

KC nodded. "When he had pneumonia."

"Right, even though he said it was just a bad cold. But he was short of staff, so he did everything but cook while he coughed and lost weight."

"He was afraid we'd lose the restaurant if he wasn't there around the clock." At last the tears began to work their way down KC's cheeks. "I called the doctor one night when he collapsed."

"Well, that's what did it, they think. The cancer grew on the scars and spread to other parts of his body."

KC tasted the salty tears running down into her mouth. "I have to stay here. I can't leave now," she said, her voice a bare whisper.

"That's right, dear," Rose said. "You better stay close to home."

KC wept in her grandmother's arms. Her eyes were hot and heavy, brimming and spilling over again and again.

Europe was very far away. But not as far as her father.

Thirteen

*L*auren picked up the filthy ashtray on the night table of Room 422 and wiped it out with her rag. After cleaning eight other rooms on the fourth floor of the Springfield Mountain Inn, she smelled like old cigarettes, mildewed towels, and bathroom cleanser.

"Hey, it's bad, but it's not that bad," she told herself. She did one last survey of the hotel room: she'd vacuumed, changed the sheets, put a new paper band across the toilet seat and new bathroom glasses on the counter, put new soap and towels and washcloths where they were supposed to be, and placed one "good night" mint on each of the two pillows. Gladys wouldn't have reason to complain this time.

Next, Lauren took her mop and stuck it in the pail on wheels, yanking it along with one hand while she shoved her laundry cart with the other. She pulled the room door shut.

I could do the next room, or I could take a break and check on who shows up to Spring Formal, she thought. Maybe she'd see someone she knew. Maybe she'd see Dash. He hated stuffy dances, but he just might "happen" to stop by. Hadn't he said he'd been thinking of coming. Maybe they'd end up talking about more than just the school newspaper.

What did she have to lose? Gladys would never know. She left all her cleaning stuff beside the next door and wandered down the hall. She could vaguely hear the band tuning up four floors below in the Powder Ballroom as she got on the elevator and pressed the lobby button. The U of S Spring Formal was about to start.

A sea of couples was strolling in. One girl was wearing a traditional prom dress, with lots of net tulle around her shoulders; another had on a skimpy silver lamé dress that barely covered her shapely figure. The two guys with them were wearing tuxes—obviously rented—and looked totally uncomfortable.

From behind the recessed wall next to the ground-floor elevator, Lauren was wondering what she would have worn when a familiar face swam into view.

It was Dash. He looked so wonderful that she nearly called out his name. He was wearing a white shirt open at the neck and a loose-fitting black jacket that really set off his dark good looks.

He didn't follow the other couples to the ballroom, but stood in the hall for a moment, as if deciding where he wanted to go next.

Lauren could feel her pulse pounding. It was so obvious to her that he couldn't have called to ask her to meet him because of his stupid pride. But if he showed up, it looked casual and offhand.

She walked out of her hiding place, her steps sure and directed right toward him.

But then the glass doors to the inn opened again. Dash turned to see who was arriving, and Lauren stood there, frozen in space as she watched him.

An incredible-looking girl stepped right up to him and took his arm. She was tall and thin, with long straight honey-blond hair that just touched her waist. She had on black flats and a black tube dress cinched in with a wide metallic belt. The belt glistened in the lights from the overhead chandeliers as the girl turned to Dash with a coy smile on her face.

He nodded to her and let her lead him down the hall, toward the ballroom.

A date. Dash was waiting for his date.

Lauren felt as if she were falling down into a pit that had no bottom. Her entire world had just crashed into tiny, unmendable pieces.

"You look sort of dreamy," Peter said. He turned KC one last time as the band in the ballroom wound down a slow number.

KC smiled up into his clear, light brown eyes. "Oh, I was just thinking about the difference between the last dance and this one. After you left me and Grandma Rose at the hotel this afternoon, I told her how Spring Formal has to make up for that awful winter formal." Several months earlier, before she had fallen in love with Peter, KC had accepted to be Peter's date at Winter Formal. But then she stood him up when a gorgeous guy asked her to go with him. Peter found out and KC had felt so shallow. Her date had been a bore and Peter had been terribly hurt.

But now it was KC who hurt. Peter didn't suspect anything was wrong. And she would see to it that he didn't. She wouldn't tell him the awful news until the evening was over.

KC applauded the band along with everyone else, keeping a smile on her face. Her shining gray eyes reflected glimpses of the mylar balloons that had been hung from the ceiling. The rest of the ballroom had yards of blue velvet draped over the walls, a mirror ball that spun above all the heads, and strings of little white Christmas lights that winked on and off everywhere.

KC looked down at her body as though it belonged to someone else. Surely it wasn't KC wearing this dress that Courtney had loaned her. It had a black top with spaghetti straps covered with black sequins and a black-and-gold skating skirt that swished across her black-stockinged thighs when she moved. KC couldn't help thinking how amazing it was that you could cover up the churning feelings inside yourself with a flashy outfit on the outside.

"How about a glass of punch?" Peter asked, starting to lead her over to the refreshments table.

"I'd love one," KC said. She hoped he wouldn't ask if she wanted something to eat. She couldn't swallow a thing.

The evening had to be special, something she could remember forever. She and Peter had to have the best time of their lives tonight. And then, afterward, she'd tell him good-bye.

It was funny how everything had changed so quickly—for her, for her father, for Peter, who was about to cross the Atlantic Ocean all on his own.

Peter put his hand on her waist and urged her forward in the punch line. He unbuttoned the jacket of his blue pin-striped suit. "Say, now that you mention it, Winter Formal really was a bummer. I guess if I'd been about to be crowned freshman princess and Winnie—one of my closest friends—had shoved me in the swimming pool and I had about the worst cold I'd ever had in my life, I'd consider the dance a washout," Peter said.

KC meant to laugh, but what came out was a strange noise that echoed around inside her. Those problems seemed so tiny, so insignificant compared with what she was going through now. And yet, to look at her tonight, with this wonderful guy on her arm, gazing into her eyes with such love, no one would ever have guessed that her world was falling apart.

They inched up on the line as the band swung into a power pop number. The amplifiers were so loud, it would have been impossible to carry on a conversation. The bass player, a hulking senior with hoop earrings in both ears, was leaping around the stage, shouting into the mike.

Peter was saying something in her ear, but she couldn't hear a thing. It didn't matter. She just needed to feel him close to her: the soft brush of his suit jacket on her wrist, the smell of his polished shoes, the weight of his hand on her waist. She closed her eyes and tried to memorize every sensation, to copy it on her brain indelibly so that she would have it always, even in the midst of mourning.

"I said the discos in Florence will be even louder," Peter yelled. "Really happening places, I bet."

KC nodded and took the glass of punch he offered her. How could she make herself swallow even one sip? How could she get her heart unstuck from this special person in time to let him go?

And then she realized she would have to do the same with her father. The thought made the breath catch hard in her throat.

Winnie drove very slowly and carefully up the long, dark road. All day she'd had this paranoid fear that a police car would stop her and accuse her of ripping off the Blue Whale Restaurant. The truth was, it would have been a relief to get caught.

She jerked along in third gear toward the chalet,

hoping for a clearing in the thickly overhanging trees. She'd borrowed Kimberly's car to meet Dimitri and she wasn't used to the clutch.

"I can't find this place. Maybe I should just turn back," she moaned under her breath. She was about twenty miles due north of Springfield now, and according to Dimitri's map, she had to be close. But did she really want to be here? Last night she'd wanted it, but now she wasn't sure. Maybe what she really wanted was to be back in the dorm with Josh!

But back to the dorm meant back to reality. What she needed and craved right now, this minute, was a rendezvous. The word brought up all kinds of passionate encounters in dangerous spots. Was she ready for the kind of risk that Dimitri always seemed to insist on? Was she really ready to meet a guy who was practically a stranger in the middle of nowhere and break into a house—and spend the night with him?

She ran over a pothole and the car swerved. She quickly turned the wheel. She'd passed a farm a few miles back, but since then, she hadn't seen any signs of life. Just empty open land and huge, old trees on either side.

"Have I really lost my mind?" she muttered as she pressed down on the accelerator. She had betrayed Josh by being with Dimitri—no, by simply *wanting* to be with him. But suppose she slept with Dimitri? What would that mean tonight, tomorrow, and for the rest of her life? She would never again be able to look Josh in the eyes and expect him to care for her.

It wasn't cold out, but she was shivering. She reached down to turn on the heat just as the car lurched over a particularly big hole. The engine stalled and ground to a halt.

Winnie pounded hard on the steering wheel, then turned the ignition on again. Reluctantly, the car started, and as she stepped on the gas it crept slowly up the road.

"Maybe this is a sign," she said to herself. "Maybe I shouldn't be here at all. Josh would be absolutely out of his mind if he knew."

Winnie drove slower now, inching along in second gear. Her second thoughts were turning into third and fourth thoughts. This was insane—driving all by herself in the middle of the night over ground that felt like the surface of the moon. And for what? To spend time with this totally out-of-control guy who made her do all kinds of things she didn't think she should be doing.

Winnie put her foot on the brake and the car moaned to a stop. She turned the engine off, then sat there in the middle of the road, staring into the pitch darkness. Why was she here if she loved Josh? Did she love Josh? Yes, absolutely. So was it just to prove something to him? To get him to look at her differently? How could she do this to Josh? He would never do anything like this to her.

Winnie felt sick to her stomach.

"I don't know what to do," she said to the night sky. "Somebody tell me what to do."

Winnie looked around frantically in the darkness, hoping to see something—a sign, a marker on the road. It was desolate and isolated out here, just as it was inside her head.

She wanted excitement—well, now she had it. Dimitri made her feel rich inside, like she was more than a mere mortal, with dull thoughts and ideas.

Winnie bit her lip hard as she turned the key in the ignition once more. The car roared to action and she charged up the hill. There it was, the final turn in the road Dimitri had described to her. The chalet—and her rendezvous—were waiting for her.

Go wild, just this once. That was what her feelings were telling her.

"Yes!" she called out loud. Her voice was the only sound in the still night.

Fourteen

"Great, now I'm lost," Faith grumbled, staring at the row of doors along the basement corridor of the Springfield Mountain Inn. "Lauren, if you want this letter Kimberly gave me for you, you better come out of one of these rooms and show yourself." She had been wandering around here for the past ten minutes without seeing one single person or having any clue where the laundry room might be. All she could hear was the pounding beat coming from the spring formal in the ballroom upstairs.

It was like a vast maze down here. Maybe she'd open one door and a fairy godmother would pop out and say, "Faith, dear, Scott's arrived to take you to the ball."

But then, with Faith's luck, the fairy would probably vanish before she could turn Faith's baggy jeans into a jazzy party dress and let her know where to find Scott. She'd have to wear a pumpkin to the ball—if Liza wasn't using it for a costume piece or Max hadn't chewed it up.

At last she saw a door that looked different from the others. It had to be the laundry room.

"Lauren, open," she said, knocking on a beige slab of steel.

The door opened, and Faith nearly fell into her friend's arms.

"Hey! You're just the person I wanted to see," Lauren said. She looked exhausted, but definitely relieved that Faith was there.

"I brought you a letter. It came to the dorm for you," Faith told her, raising her voice slightly over the rumble of the machines.

She walked past her friend into the laundry room, a small cubicle lined with shelves that held soap, bleach, and softener. There was an ironing board smack in the middle of the room and a pile of men's shirts, ready to be sprinkled, in a basket by the side of the board. The four walls were lined with washers and dryers.

"Boy, it's as hot in here as it is cold in the trap room," Faith complained, sitting on the only available chair, an orange plastic molded one that was just as uncomfortable as it looked.

Lauren stared at her friend's clothes as she sat down on the floor beside her. "You're not going to the dance?"

Faith shook her head.

"What happened to Scott?"

"He had a game. Couldn't make it," Faith said. She started picking apart her braid. First one strand of hair, then the next. "We were leaving things loose, and I said that was fine—but I have to admit that it's totally un-fine. If just one thing I wanted could have worked out . . ."

Lauren got up and hugged Faith. "So you and I don't have dates," she said. "It's not the end of the world."

Faith noticed deep shadows under Lauren's violet eyes. Laura looked as miserable as Faith felt. "Boy, I wish we were living together again," Faith said with a heavy sigh.

"Me too," Lauren agreed. "I feel so alone in my apartment. I wish I'd never moved off campus now."

"You didn't have a choice," Faith said. "But speaking of your former dwelling place, I've got a letter that came for you today." She took an envelope out of her pocket and handed it to Lauren. "I actually came here to give it to you. Maybe it's good news."

Lauren took it and stared hard at the handwriting. She made a face, then, almost reluctantly, she ripped open the flap. "I can tell what's going to be in here," she said as she unfolded the small, cream-colored note. "And it won't be good news." Then she read the note, and read it a second time.

"What is it?" Faith asked.

Lauren kept staring at the letter, dumbfounded.

"Lauren! Tell me!"

Lauren still didn't answer. Instead she started laughing. She laughed so hard, tears rolled down her cheeks.

Faith looked at her as though she'd gone nuts. "What *is* it?"

Lauren handed the note to Faith. Faith began to read aloud.

Dear Lauren

    As you know, your mother was terribly upset by your decision not to pledge a sorority. She felt that you had squandered a golden opportunity that might have given you a real start in life. She convinced me that you ought to be taught a lesson.

    Frankly, I thought you would leave school

and come back home after we froze your trust fund. I guess that's the sort of thing I would have done, way back when I was your age.

But it turns out, my daughter has a lot more spine than I ever did. You stuck it out, you made do with what you had, you didn't complain. You wanted to stay at the University of Springfield, regardless of what it cost you—in feelings as well as in dollars and cents.

And I am proud of you. I want you to know that as of today, the papers restoring your trust are in the mail to our lawyer. We all make a lot of mistakes in this life, but luckily, we often seem to get a second chance. I'm glad I've had the chance to give you back what's rightfully yours.

Love, Dad

Faith looked up from the note. "Oh, my goodness!" She shook the paper in Lauren's face. "You've got your trust back! You're rich!"

Lauren folded her arms in front of her chest. "You know, I've had a hundred conversations with my folks in my mind before I go to sleep," she said. "And every single time, I tell them the money isn't that important to me—it's getting back together with them." Suddenly there were tears shining in her eyes. "Faith, my dad still cares about me."

This time Faith got up and put her arms around Lauren. "I'm sure, he always did."

Lauren nodded, and was very quiet for a minute, her eyes focused on some point in space.

Faith made a fist and raised it high in the air. Then she gave a whoop and started leaping around the room. "No more maid job! You can quit right now!"

Lauren spun in a circle. "You're right. Oh, I can't wait to tell Gladys to stick her head in a pail. And I can't wait to tell my rotten landlord to go take a running dive. I can move back on campus!"

Faith rubbed her hands together. "Well, what are we waiting for? Get that stupid cleaning outfit off and let's go celebrate. I for one feel like devouring a hot fudge sundae." She grabbed the door of the laundry room and yanked it open.

Lauren already had her apron off and was working on the suspender straps. "Who needs Spring Formal?" she said. "Who needs dates? We're going to have more fun than anyone we know."

Together they ran down the corridor, laughing hysterically, happier than they'd both been in weeks.

Melissa stopped dancing. She shook her head and lifted one foot in the air and massaged it as a signal to Brooks that her feet were killing her. Brooks nodded and let her lead him off the dance floor.

"Do you mind if we sit a few out?" Melissa asked when they were finally out of the range of the band's incredible amplification.

Brooks shrugged. "Sure. What do you want to do? Are you hungry?"

It would have been easy to say yes. To go eat dinner with a few other couples. To do a whole cover-up again of all the feelings that were jumping around inside her. But she couldn't take the easy way out—not this time.

"How about we go down to the pool and dangle our feet in the water?" Melissa suggested. She figured it would be quiet there. If they had to yell and scream, no one else would hear.

Brooks took her hand and together they walked out of the ballroom, down the hall toward the pool. As they opened the door the steamy smell of chlorine hit them.

The place was empty. Melissa knew she had no more excuses.

Brooks grabbed two kickboards for them to sit on and brought them down to the shallow end. They both kicked off their shoes, and Melissa hiked up the satin plaid skirt she had on until it sat in a stiff cloud over her knees. She hadn't worn stockings, so she just let her bare feet flop into the water.

"Nice dance," Brooks murmured.

"You don't think it's nice at all," she said softly. "You think it stinks."

He turned to her puzzled, his eyebrows knit together. "What do you mean?"

"You're having a rotten time and so am I," she went on calmly. So far, this was easier than she thought. But she hadn't gotten to the tough part yet.

"Actually," Brooks said, "I suppose you're right. I wasn't really in the mood for a dance tonight." He stared moodily into the water, and she thought, at last, that she could read a little of what was going through his mind.

"Oh, Brooks, I have to apologize," she began. She put a hand on his shoulder, then took it off again when he didn't even turn to her.

"About what?"

"About how I've been avoiding everything. Mostly you."

Suddenly she heard him breathe. Then breathe again. "Yeah."

"It's not that I don't want to talk to you. I just get so scared sometimes that I'm going to botch it. I open my mouth to say what I feel, and out come theorems, formulas, the number of bones in your left hand."

Brooks leaned toward her. "Melissa, I'm really glad to hear you saying this. I was beginning to think—"

"—that I didn't love you!" Melissa finished for him. "Oh, I know you thought that. But Brooks, I love you so much." She swung her legs out of the water and got up on her knees on the kickboard so that she could look into his strong, honest face. "I care more than you'll ever know."

Brooks stroked her copper hair, and she could smell the good clean soapy smell that always made her feel content around him.

"I think we'll make it, Mel," he said finally. "As long as you keep on trying like this, we'll make it."

"I promise to keep talking," she said. "Even if it hurts sometimes." She turned her face up to his. "I want us to get married and stay married and be that way for the rest of our lives."

"Me too," he said, and he kissed her.

The dance was over and the musicians were packing up their instruments, but KC couldn't move. She held an empty glass in her hands and twirled a straw inside it. This corner table seemed safe to her. As long as she sat there she could make the evening last longer. She could think about the last two hours when she and Peter had barely spoken, but instead had simply moved together, two bodies becoming one. His hands touching hers, their heads close, breathing in sync. She needed these last precious moments.

"I guess we're going to close up the inn tonight," Peter joked. The waiters were clearing plates and glasses and the dance committee was taking the strings of pinlights off the walls. But KC just sat there.

"I know you hate the idea of starting real life over again tomorrow, but them's the breaks," Peter said. "We gotta finish packing. We gotta go over our lists. We gotta fly to Italy. We gotta go, KC." He took her hands and yanked her out of her seat.

She stood there unsteadily, thinking that her life was ending. This wonderful evening and the fabulous person beside her were the very best she had ever had. She would never in her life know this kind of happiness again.

"Peter?" she began.

"Yes?" His deep blue eyes peered into hers.

They were practically knocked aside by two burly waiters who had chosen just that moment to start moving and stacking the tables. "You guys mind?" said one waiter. "The formal's over."

"Sure," Peter said good-naturedly. He took KC around the waist and guided her to the door of the ballroom. "I promise I'll find you some super dance in Florence to go to. Some countess's ball, how's that?"

KC burst into tears.

"What is it?" Peter asked, pressing her close. "Did I say something wrong?" He moved away from her, but she clung to him, making it impossible for him to see into her sad eyes. "KC, what's upsetting you like this? I can understand feeling kind of blue when you're leaving friends, but we're beginning a wonderful adventure. You'll be homesick, sure. But it's not like you'll never see your family and friends again. Everyone is rooting for you—your dad and mom and grandma and Winnie and Faith and Courtney and—"

KC pulled away from him and started running down the hall, running away from everything she had to think about the next day, and the next.

Peter, however, ran faster, and caught her just as she reached the front door of the Springfield Inn. He led her outside, onto the wide columned veranda that spread around the inn. Drawing her toward the railing, he leaned her up against it.

"You have to talk to me. Just say it. I'm here for you."

KC nodded, but she didn't stop crying. The tears flowed freely even as she spoke. "I'm not going to Europe with you," she said in a low voice.

"What are you talking about? Of course you are."

"Peter, something bad—" She couldn't finish.

"Your grandmother . . . oh, no, don't tell me you were right?"

"No, it's not Rose. She was here to see the doctors at the hospital about my . . . my father's tests," she blurted out. "If I go to Italy, I may never see him again." She started to sob.

Peter pulled her close again and let her weep against his shoulder. "KC, what is it?"

She didn't answer for a long time. Then she spit it out. "Cancer. My father has lung cancer, Peter."

Peter looked as if someone had drained all the blood from his body. Finally he spoke. "KC, I want to be with you while you're going through this. I don't know how to help—I don't even know what to say—but I'm not going anywhere. I'm staying here with you."

"It's not what you're meant to do, Peter," KC said simply. "We have to be in different places now."

He started to cry. "I can't go without you."

KC's fingers softly wiped the tears off his cheeks. "I'd hate myself for keeping you chained to me. You have to go to Italy, for both of us."

They kissed, and all the unhappiness they each felt was touched with a new feeling. A bonding. They could never be split apart now.

"I would do anything to make your father well again."

She nodded. "But that can't happen."

"KC," he whispered into her hair, "I love you."

"And I love you. You're not going to be very far away from me, because you're inside me wherever I am."

They held each other tightly, and when the sun came up an hour later, they were still there, locked in each other's arms.

Fifteen

The chalet came into view, silhouetted against the dark sky, as Winnie took the last turn in the road. She'd arrived.

"Turn around, you idiot. Go back," she pleaded with herself, but her hands felt welded to the steering wheel, her foot unable to get off the accelerator. It was harder going now, uphill, but the car was suddenly behaving. It seemed to want her to go through with her risk-filled rendezvous.

The car tires crunched on the rocks and gravel at the end of the drive. Winnie eased her foot off the gas pedal and applied the brake. She came to a halt and for the next few minutes she sat in the car with the lights out, listening to the engine humming as it cooled off. She, on the other hand, was all heated up inside, all cylinders firing at once. She was like a runaway train, barreling through the night toward an unknown place. All she knew was that she had to get there, even if she crashed.

The chalet was surrounded by huge oak trees. It had fancy wooden decks with gingerbread detail on two levels and slate steps leading up to a huge wooden door with a big knocker. It wasn't that large, but it hovered over the landscape because it was the only building among all these trees.

Had Dimitri already picked the lock and broken in? Was he waiting for her inside? The thought made her skin tingle.

She imagined going to the door—which would be slightly ajar. She'd step inside and whisper, "Dimitri?" And she'd hear him sigh, feel his warm breath on her neck. Then his hands would gather around her waist, and his mouth would meet hers. And she'd be totally lost, unable to stop.

The sky was strange and wild, just like her, with patterns of clouds racing over the faint crescent moon. A storm was brewing. The trees shivered under a gust of wind.

Winnie opened the door and stepped out of the car.

The shape of a tall, well-built man loomed by the side of the house, beneath a window. He didn't move, but she could feel his presence. Goose bumps covered her skin, and she was having trouble breathing.

If you do this, Winnie, you're a different person. Not a good person.

But how could she not reach out and grab what was in front of her? She walked toward him, anticipating everything, trying to regret nothing. She heard her shoes kicking the pebbles as she made her way up the path to the house. Every step led closer to Dimitri, and further from Josh.

She stopped about five yards from him and wiped her sweaty palms on her short jean skirt. She felt so exposed suddenly, in this skirt and the black halter top with her little patchwork jacket over it. She felt as if she needed to drape herself in a big sheet to cover up.

"Hi," he whispered.

"Hi." She took one more step—the last step, from which there was no going back.

"How was the drive up?"

Winnie blinked, peering into the darkness. The voice didn't sound like Dimitri's. It sounded like a voice she knew almost as well as her own.

"Josh?"

"Yeah, it's me."

Her mind raced. Her feet felt fixed in place. She couldn't move foward or back. "What in the world . . . ?"

He edged closer to her. She could see his dark hair, blown around a little by the breeeze, and just make out the blue marble dot of an earring on his right ear. He had on the polo shirt she'd given him for his birthday, with all those buttons down the front that he complained were constantly coming off. She could see his eyes asking her whether it was all right for him to be here.

"Winnie, do you still want me?" he asked softly.

Winnie suddenly crumbled inside. The very fact that he was asking meant that he knew about Dimitri—that she'd hurt him terribly. Her eyes started to fill with tears.

"I'm so glad you're here, Josh!" she said.

"You didn't answer my question." Josh took her hand, led her to the steps in front of the chalet, and drew her down beside him.

"Yes, I still want you."

"So what are we going to do, Winnie Gottlieb?" Josh asked, moving away so that they weren't touching anymore. "You need to go out with other people and I need to put my work ahead of my being in love with you."

Winnie couldn't help it. She started crying. It was

the way he said the word *love,* with such strength and commitment. He had loved her all the time, when she was running around trying to find Dimitri in the lab, when she was going out to a fancy restaurant and climbing out the window so they didn't have to pay, when she was nearly getting herself killed walking around a tower ledge, when she was driving up here to cheat on him. He loved her all that time.

"Don't cry. Crying won't fix anything." He put an arm around her shoulders. Awkwardly, as if for the first time, they drew closer. Then she turned her face to him. He meant to kiss her mouth, but she moved and he got her chin instead.

Even though it was dark, she could see him as though it were broad daylight. The knowing green eyes, the slightly large nose, the mouth with its full lips.

"Josh, I have to tell you everything."

"Good. Then I'll tell you a few things."

She exhaled, then leaned back against the wobbly steps.

"I met this guy running—"

"Dimitri."

"Yeah, and he was incredible. Not that you're not incredible," she quickly corrected herself, putting a hand on his knee and leaving it there because he let her. "But he challenged me to do things I thought I couldn't do, and he made me feel, I don't know, *new* inside."

"Which I don't," Josh said, a real sorrow in his voice.

"No. Yes." Winnie stuck her face in her hands and rubbed it hard, hoping some true answers would come out faster.

Josh got up and walked toward the small, untended garden that flanked the chalet. Winnie could see how tense his body was. "Maybe I'm not the right guy for you, Winnie. Maybe I'm too rooted in ordinary, everyday—"

"That's not true!" Winnie said. She jumped up and ran to him, grabbing him around the waist. "I always want to be with you. When I'm not with you, I'm thinking about you."

Josh pulled away from her again, as though he were too close for comfort. "Look, I saw you and this guy, Dimitri, in the restaurant last night, and I was sure it was all over between us. I don't ever remember feeling so bad in all my life."

"I'm sorry," she said in a very small voice.

"Sorry. Well, I am, too. We should both be sorry. I tell you, I saw how cozy you two were in the restaurant and I thought, why aren't *we* like that? Were we ever? Did we lose something?"

She was very quiet, feeling desperate to put all the broken pieces back together and not knowing how to do it.

Josh shook his head. "I thought that what we had was carved in stone, couldn't be changed." He picked up a pebble and threw it hard at a tree.

Winnie touched his shoulder. "Nothing real should be made out of stone. It has to be able to grow."

"I know that now."

She was glad he couldn't really see her face in the dark. There was so much pain in it, so much terror that he was going to say no, they really shouldn't be a couple. That he'd decided it was over.

Josh picked up another stone. He held it and rubbed it, as if for luck. "Then I thought, what am I doing to drive her over the brink?"

"And what did you decide?" she asked softly.

"I decided that life's too short. Sure, my assignments are important, but caring for you is more important. How many other people do we know who have what we've got? You throw that away, you might as well be dead and buried."

Winnie couldn't stand not touching him. She threw her arms around his neck and pulled him to her. His belt buckle clinked with the buckle on her jean skirt. She was never going to let Josh go. She was just going to stand here with him until the end of time.

"Well," he said into her ear, softly stroking her back, "I figured I had to take the next step. I found Dimitri this morning and explained that you and I were a couple. It didn't matter what had gone on between the two of you, but I had to have the chance to win you back. He told me where to meet you tonight. And here I am."

Winnie felt a rush of energy. Josh wanted her. Josh was forgiving her! The tears started coming again and she pressed close to him, murmuring, "I promise, Josh, I'll never hurt you again."

A growl came from deep within him and he lifted her off her feet, crushing her close in a tight embrace. "Neither will I. Win, you're like part of me. When you're not around, I'm not whole."

They wanted each other so badly. Everything that had ever come between them was evaporating, and they could start again. It was like dawn, Winnie thought, when that red ball comes over the horizon and the sky suddenly drinks it in. She leaned forward, and he met her lips. They clung together, hanging on to each other, and the kiss was so sweet and so thrilling that Winnie wondered how she had been able to go without one for so long.

After a while they drew back, both breathing hard.

"Let's not stay out here," Josh whispered. "We could go inside."

The chalet. She'd almost forgotten. They had to leave before someone caught them snooping around the property. "No, we can't go inside."

"All right. But I can't wait to get home, Winnie. I want to be with you, hold you, touch you. Right here and now."

Winnie was trembling with all the love that brimmed up in her, and so excited it was difficult to walk.

The wind suddenly came up and the window-panes of the old house began to rattle. It started to rain lightly. Winnie pulled her hand from Josh's and backed down the steps. "No breaking and entering. Not for you and me," she said. She didn't need thrills like that anymore. She had Josh back, and that was thrill enough for her. "But I want you, too. Where can we go?"

"I know. You remember River Run Lodge, that crazy old place we passed when we were looking for somewhere for your mom to stay?"

"The one with those little cabins with fire-places?"

Josh nodded and pulled her close again. "We can

rent one for the night. We won't go to sleep. Just hold each other in front of the fire and forget everything and everyone else."

Winnie felt delirious. Josh wanted her, really wanted to be with her. "Should we be ourselves?" Winnie asked, pulling at a lock of his dark hair. "Or be different people, a new couple with a whole new love affair?"

"Sure," he agreed. "We can pretend to be acrobats from Eastern Europe."

Winnie giggled. "Or we could be hicks from some tiny mountain town, just passing through. We could offer to split a few logs for a night's lodging."

A bolt of lightning shot through the sky, and Josh grabbed her hand. "We've got to get out of here!"

They ran together to Kimberly's car, and Josh pushed her inside and shut the door. Then he shifted closer to her on the seat. "We won't have time to split logs," he whispered in her ear. "We'll be too busy being in love." He kissed her again as the thunder boomed outside.

"We go together, you know," he said, leaning his head against her. "Like bread and butter. No, better than that—like you and me."

They didn't need Spring Formal. They didn't need anything but one another. Winnie leaned back in his arms and saw her whole life starting right at that moment. They would be wild and crazy sometimes. Other times, down-to-earth and sensible. But always and foremost, they would be together.

Nothing—and no one—else mattered.

Sixteen

"Park here! No, over here!" Faith said, laughing. She held on to the Jeep's dashboard as Lauren steered her new vehicle in a huge circle around the parking lot outside Forest Hall, then backed it up and made a reverse circle.

Three guys were just coming out of the dorm and stood cheering them. Lauren finally pulled into a spot by the side door. "Way to go!" one of the guys yelled.

"Hey, you don't drive like a girl," another exclaimed.

Lauren frowned at him as she pulled up on the

emergency brake and took the keys out of the ignition. "I'm not a girl. I'm a woman," she stated proudly.

Lauren was feeling wonderful. Only a week ago she'd been sitting in the laundry room at the Springfield Inn feeling sorry for herself. And now, with her family on her good side and her trust fund back in commission, she was her old self again.

She'd gotten a new haircut, had bought presents for all her friends, and gotten herself a few things as well. Today she was wearing her new baggy silk pants and the little brocaded jacket with frog buttons that she'd bought at the funkiest shop in Springfield. The best thing, though, was that she'd had three good phone conversations with her father and one with her mother.

"You think Winnie's still around?" she asked as she locked the door of the Jeep.

Faith jumped out of the car and shut the door on the passenger side. "I hope so. I know she was going to see Josh sometime today, but maybe we'll catch her in." They walked along the winding path toward the dorm.

Lauren grinned. "You really think Winnie and I would get along as roommates?" she asked. "That is *if* Melissa and Brooks get married and Mel moves out of the dorm."

"Hey, Winnie's a wonder. You'd love living with her."

"Not as much as I'd love to live with you," Lauren said. "I guess there's no budging Liza."

"Nope," Faith agreed with a disgusted smirk. "Liza may hate me, but she's not about to move anytime soon. At least if you live on campus again, it'll make things bearable."

"For me, too. You and I could spend lots more time together. How about going shopping tomorrow?" she asked as they reached the door of the dorm and she pulled it open.

"Lauren! We've shopped till we've dropped!" Faith protested.

"But we only replaced the things that got spilled on or chewed," Lauren pointed out. "That's not enough."

"It's more than enough," Faith said, giving her friend's hand a squeeze. She had on her old jeans from high school *and*, thanks to Lauren's generosity, a fabulous pair of high suede boots with silver tips that matched her new suede jacket. She was carrying a distressed-leather satchel that served as a book bag.

"I don't know." Lauren shook her head, feeling really pleased that she could do something for her friend. "You may need another little something somewhere down the line. But we can deal with that."

They walked into the lounge, where two jocks were playing Ping-Pong and another was watching TV. Lauren felt like skipping. The whole atmosphere was so different from her dreary little apartment off campus. She decided she really liked people. It was nice having them around and being around them.

A guy with a shock of black hair and a two-day beard walked through the lounge, and suddenly, without meaning to, Lauren found herself thinking about Dash again. She really wanted to tell him what was going on. Except after seeing him with the girl at the formal, she didn't know where she stood. Or where he stood.

And even though Lauren had tried hanging around the U-of -S *Weekly Journal* office when she turned in her *Hers* column, he didn't show. She just hoped he'd read the column soon and call her about it. She'd directed the whole thing—about lack of communication between men and women—right to him. If it had no effect, she decided, she was a pretty lousy writer.

"Look! There's Winnie!" Faith said when they pulled open the stairwell door of the second floor.

Lauren snapped out of her daydream about Dash.

"Hey, Winnie!" Faith called. "It's us." She dragged Lauren down the long corridor to Room 152, where Winnie was standing at the door holding the doorknob of her room in one hand and staring into space.

Winnie smiled happily. "I'm not going anywhere," she said. "As a matter of fact, I'm locked out." She held up the doorknob. "Maybe it's fate. Maybe I'll have to move in with Josh."

Faith laughed and shook her head. "Fate, as an important factor in *Macbeth* and the life of Winnie Gottlieb."

"We could do a term paper on it," Winnie agreed cheerily. Then she stopped and looked at Lauren. "Boy, do you look great! Can I borrow that outfit sometime?" Winnie took Lauren by the shoulders and turned her from one side to the other. "As a matter of fact, you look like a whole different person."

Lauren smiled. "Thanks. I'm feeling on top of the world. Listen, I bet I can fix this. After living in the Disaster Arms Apartments, I had to learn to fix anything. My super never did."

She fitted the knob into its circle and started turning it until it clicked into place. Then she pressed in, and bingo, the door opened.

Winnie dropped her jaw in amazement. "Wow!

Can you make beds, too? Maybe I should get you as a roommate."

Lauren and Faith exchanged glances. "That's exactly what we were both thinking," Faith said. "Have Brooks and Melissa set a date yet? Do you know when she's moving out?"

Winnie shrugged. "Melissa hasn't said anything to me. But as soon as she moves out you're moving in, Lauren. Come on, I'll give you the two-cent tour."

She led the girls into the room and hastily swept clothing, running shoes, books, and a couple of tapes off her unmade bed. "You will note the lovely orange racing stripes on the overhead molding in dramatic contrast to the white stucco ceilings. We also have sturdy motel-quality walls, guaranteed to give you the best eavesdropping capability this side of Washington, D.C." She went over to her desk and picked up a U-of-S coffee mug, which she placed against the plasterboard. She put her ear to the mug and listened, pretending to be shocked.

Then she straightened up, spreading her arms out to show off all the features she'd mentioned. "You like it? It's yours. Well, half of it, anyway."

Lauren hugged herself. "Oh, Winnie. I love it. Anytime, day or night, call me if it's free."

"You bet. I think we'd make a great pair. We'll

talk about it as soon as I pin Melissa down."

Faith elbowed Lauren in the side. "I told you so."

"Yeah. It's all settled," Winnie said. "Now I'd invite you guys to stay awhile, but I have a date with somebody down the hall," she told them. "He'll be knocking on my door any minute."

"We get the message," Faith said. "C'mon Lauren, let's scram."

They were almost out the door when Lauren turned and walked over to Winnie's desk. The bulletin board above it was hanging down on one side and Lauren quickly took a dictionary out of the book ends on the shelf and used it to pound the loose tack back into the wall. Then she straightened the bulletin board.

Winnie doubled over. "How have I been able to live without you, Lauren?" she asked.

"Beats me," Lauren said. "Bye, see you later."

"Well, it's about time you showed up," Winnie said, pulling the door open the rest of the way. But she was startled to see just who was on the other side.

"Dimitri!"

She hadn't seen him since their climb out onto

the ledge of the tower and she didn't really know what to say.

"Listen, you were great about the other night," she blurted out. "It was, well, generous of you to fix things up with me and Josh. I wanted to thank you. I should have come and found you and told you how much I appreciate—"

Dimitri held up a hand. "Wait! Let's not make me out to be Saint Francis, okay?" he said in his musical accent. "Josh hunted me down and told me how things stood between you two. I respected him for it. I'm not into breaking up tight couples. I hope you've patched things up." He stuck out his hand. "No hard feelings?"

She smiled at him and put her hand in his. "No hard feelings. Just good ones. I really owe you for this."

He gave her one of his sexy lopsided smiles that always made her melt. Only this time, oddly enough, she found that it didn't have the desired effect. Now that she had Josh back, she could look at him differently. She had perspective.

"Well, I tell you," he said, turning her hand over in his and tracing the lines on her palm. "Maybe there is something you could do for me."

"Sure. Anything. You name it."

He drew up one side of her life line, then down

her love line. "I saw this dynamite girl outside getting into a new Jeep. You know her?"

Winnie started to laugh. "Lauren? She may just be my next roommate. You want to meet her?"

He winked. "As soon as possible."

"It's a deal," Winnie said.

"Okay, so I'll see you. You're one in a million," he told her. He lifted her hand and kissed it, then gave her a mock salute and started to leave. Suddenly he turned, as though he'd forgotten something. "You will probably be happy to know I had a friend drop off an envelope for me at the Blue Whale. No names. Just cash. I think they'll understand, don't you?"

Before she could tell him how relieved she was, Dimitri was out the door, whistling as he strolled down the hall. Winnie couldn't make out the tune, but it was a lilting, bouncy melody that let her know she really hadn't hurt him in any way.

She smiled to herself and followed Dimitri out, coming to a stop just five doors away.

She threw open the door to Josh's room. "I couldn't wait anymore." Then she stopped. She couldn't believe it. Josh was doing it again. He was glued to that green screen and he was writing so fast, his fingers were a blur on the keyboard.

"That's okay," he said. "I'm a little late because

I had to turn this monster on and type a list of things that you and I have to do. Trips to take, movies to see, food to eat, plans to make." He swiveled around in his seat and held out his arms.

Winnie came to him quickly, and when he stood up and gathered her into his embrace, she thought that she had never in her life felt anything as strong as the beat of their two hearts touching.

"I want to kiss you for a long time," he whispered in her ear.

"I've got a few minutes," she told him, linking her fingers into his belt loops.

And then they didn't speak again until his computer started whirring and groaning.

Lazily, Winnie drew her mouth away from his. "Aren't you going to check on that?" she murmured.

Josh pulled her even closer. "Uh-uh."

"Don't you think something might be wrong?"

"Winnie, nothing's wrong here. Now, can't we concentrate on what we were doing?"

Winnie laughed. "Okay." And they kissed again.

Here's a sneak preview of Freshman Feud, the sixteenth book in the compelling story of FRESHMAN DORM.

KC felt like her head was going to explode. She'd spent the day cooped up in her tiny dorm room at Langston House, worrying. Worrying about her father's cancer. Worrying about her boyfriend, Peter, who was in Italy, half a world away. And worrying about her term paper that was due the next morning. KC knew if she didn't do something to clear her head, and do it soon, she'd come unglued.

"I've got to get out of here and go somewhere—anywhere," KC murmured as she grabbed a jacket and threw open the door to her room.

She hurried down the staircase and out onto the dorm green. The cool air felt good against her face. Taking deep breaths, KC walked slowly, trying to relax. Several students on bicycles pedaled past her on their way to the U of S library. To her left, a couple was huddled together on one of the wooden benches, giggling as they shared an ice-cream cone. KC walked on until she noticed a bank of phones lining the sidewalk. Suddenly she was seized with an uncontrollable urge to call home.

Her head throbbed as she slipped coins into the pay phone and dialed. She carefully massaged her temple with two fingers as she waited for someone to answer.

"Oh, KC, it's you." Her grandmother's voice sounded tired. "I thought it might be the hospital."

KC felt her stomach clench into one giant knot of fear. "Why? What's the matter? Is Dad okay?"

"He's fine," her grandmother reassured her. "Just as stubborn as ever, darn him. Everyone, and I mean *everyone*, including your mother and all the doctors, has tried to talk him into doing chemotherapy, but he still refuses. I told him—"

"But why would the hospital be calling?" KC interrupted.

"He went in for a few more tests today to see if

the high-keratin diet he put himself on has had any positive effect. They said they'd call as soon as they had the test results."

"Oh." KC breathed a deep sigh of relief and leaned back against the plastic shell of the phone booth. "I hope it's working."

"I hope so, too, Kahia." The anger and frustration in her grandmother's voice drained away into a defeated monotone. "I've never understood his health-food mania, but if that's how he intends to fight this thing, then I'll stick by him."

Her grandmother didn't say the words, "till the end," but the feeling was there. A huge lump formed in KC's throat and she could barely choke out, "Is Dad home now?"

"Yes, but he's gone to bed early and your mother is at the restaurant," Grandma Rose said. "Do you want me to wake him?"

"No, that's okay. Just tell him that I called and that I love him."

When KC hung up the phone, it took a full five minutes for her to compose herself. She took deep breaths again, trying not to cry, but little hiccuping sobs kept escaping from her throat.

There was nothing she could do about her father, but school was another matter. She groaned as she glanced at her watch. The term paper was due tomorrow at 8:45 A.M. and she hadn't spent one second working on it. KC had let that assignment and most of her other homework slide because she thought she'd be leaving mid-semester. Now everything had changed, and she was about to face the prospect of failing the one class from her declared major.

KC checked her watch. "Nine o'clock," she muttered to herself. "I have almost exactly twelve hours to write my paper."

All wasn't completely lost. She had chosen her title—*Business Practices in the Workplace: Japan vs. America.* And she'd even read a few magazine articles on the subject and made some notes on five-by-seven cards. If KC worked nonstop, she might be able to finish the paper by morning.

Can I do it? she wondered, wiping at the mascara streaks she knew had gathered under her eyes. I've got to.

With new determination KC hurried across the dorm green toward Langston House. But the closer she got to the weathered old dorm with the wraparound porch, the less confident she felt. By the time she'd climbed the big oak staircase to her room, she was exhausted—physically and mentally. Images of Peter and her father kept filling her head, blocking out any coherent thoughts about Japanese business practices.

KC opened the door to her room. The bed with its quilt from home looked more inviting than ever.

"If I could just rest my eyes for a few minutes, I might be able to think more clearly," KC said, slumping down on the edge of the narrow bed.

Then she caught sight of her reflection in the mirror.

"Oh, God. I look terrible." KC's attempts to wipe away her smeared makeup had only made things worse. It was clear that what she really needed was a brisk shower.

KC slipped out of her clothes and into her terry cloth robe. She grabbed the pale pink towel from its hook on the back of her closet door and shuffled down the hall. As she slipped into the bathroom, KC was unaware that someone was watching her.

Marielle Danner arrived at Langston House just in time to catch KC coming out of her room. Seeing a dejected and disheveled KC perked up Marielle's spirits, which were seriously sagging after the frustrating evening she'd spent with her boyfriend.

Mark Geisslinger was in charge of ODT's

Thursday slate of activities for Greek Week and had talked of nothing else all night. It was really starting to get on Marielle's nerves. In fact, Mark's frat activities had become a major bone of contention between them, ever since she'd been kicked out of the Tri Betas.

"If I hear one more mention of Greek Week," she'd told Mark during dinner at the Blue Whale, "I think I'll scream."

Mark had been completely unsympathetic. "You're just jealous that you're not a part of it," he'd said.

"It's not jealousy," she'd fumed. "It's anger. I'm mad as hell that high and mighty Courtney Conner wrapped the entire Tri Beta house around her little finger and got them to turn against me. She's no better than I am."

"That's right," Mark had said, nuzzling her neck suggestively. "And I know for a fact that you're the best."

Marielle had given him an angry shove. With Mark, everything came back to sex. "That's not what I'm talking about and you know it."

Mark had thrown his napkin on the table. "Look, if that's the way you feel," he'd snapped, "maybe we shouldn't see each other until this week is over."

"Maybe we shouldn't," Marielle had shot back.

The return drive to Langston House had been in silence, allowing thoughts of Courtney, the Tri Betas, and revenge to swirl in Marielle's head.

This was why she was smiling now. Marielle knew KC was the key to getting her revenge on Courtney Conner. And tonight was as good a time as any to get to work on KC's downfall.

After a quick stop in her room for her makeup kit, Marielle hurried into the bathroom. The water was already running in the shower. Marielle positioned herself by the sinks so that KC would be sure to see her when she came out.

Five minutes later KC emerged from the shower, towel-drying her hair. Marielle faced the mirror and began carefully applying mascara to her lashes.

"Hi, KC," she called casually over her shoulder. "I didn't expect to see you home this early during Greek Week."

"I guess I'm just not up to socializing," KC mumbled as she continued to dry her hair.

Marielle brushed just a hint of mauve eye shadow on each eyelid, all the while keeping a watchful eye on KC. "I know what you mean," she said. "It's nice to be part of a sorority, and there's no denying that the Tri Betas are the best, but sometimes there're just too many people wanting to pry into your private life."

KC stopped drying her hair and stared down at

the white-tiled floor.

Marielle continued slowly. "Sometimes you just need an understanding ear to listen to your troubles without making any judgments."

KC nodded, and damp strands of hair fell across her face.

"Belonging to a sorority can make the good times better," Marielle said, "but I always found that when things got tough, the Tri Betas were just another group of people demanding something of me." She turned to face KC and said in a singsong voice, "You *have* to go to the chapter dinner, we *need* you to decorate, but *everybody's* collecting for this charity—"

"We *want* you at the dance. You *have* to make a fool of yourself begging for money," KC joined in. It felt good to get it off her chest. She continued her list of complaints. "Wear the right clothes, talk to the right people, don't gain weight—"

Marielle put her hands on her hips and said sternly, "And for God's sake, keep your grades up!"

KC winced and slumped against the sink. "Grades. You had to mention that."

"Are you having problems with school?" Marielle prodded.

"I've got a term paper due tomorrow morning

that I haven't even started." KC tugged at the little strings on her terry cloth robe, feeling the tears well up in her eyes once more. "My father's sick, my boyfriend is gone, this paper is due and I'm exhausted."

"I've got something that will perk you up," Marielle said, feeling like a cat ready to pounce on her mouse. "You won't even think about sleeping. Your head will stay clear, and you'll ace that term paper." She unzipped the side pocket of her makeup bag and pulled out a tiny brass pill box. The top was inlaid with mother-of-pearl. She clicked open the lid and held out her hand. "Meet Bennie."

KC stared at the tiny white pill resting on Marielle's palm. "What is that? Some kind of drug?"

Marielle threw her head back and laughed, a lilting laugh that rang with reassurance. "Hardly," she said. "It's just a little something to pick you up. Everyone uses bennies."

"Everyone?"

"Sure. All the students take bennies when they want to pull an all-nighter. They're called the Freshman's Friend." Marielle could see that KC wasn't convinced so she added, "Look. A bennie is like taking No-Doze, or drinking two cups of coffee, only you don't get an upset stomach and, believe me, you feel terrific. I still use them and I'm not even a freshman anymore."

KC held out her hand. "Let me look at it."

"There you go." Marielle dropped it in KC's palm. "Free of charge."

KC hesitated for only a second. Then in one swift move, she popped the pill in her mouth, flicked on the faucet, and bent forward to take a sip of water.

Behind her Marielle was smiling at her own reflection in triumph. "That-a-girl," she said, patting KC on the back. "Stick with Marielle, she knows what's best for you."